Enamored with the Bluestocking

HISTORICAL REGENCY ROMANCE NOVEL

Sally Forbes

Copyright © 2024 by Sally Forbes
All Rights Reserved.
This book may not be reproduced or transmitted in any form without the written permission of the publisher. In no way is it legal to reproduce, duplicate, or transmit any part of this document in either electronic means or in printed format. Recording of this publication is strictly prohibited and any storage of this document is not allowed unless with written permission from the publisher.

Table of Contents

Prologue 3
Chapter One 8
Chapter Two 20
Chapter Three 30
Chapter Four 41
Chapter Five 54
Chapter Six 65
Chapter Seven 75
Chapter Eight 85
Chapter Nine 94
Chapter Ten.. 102
Chapter Eleven 114
Chapter Twelve 122
Chapter Thirteen 129
Chapter Fourteen 139
Chapter Fifteen 145
Chapter Sixteen 156
Chapter Seventeen... 166
Chapter Eighteen 177
Epilogue 195

Prologue

"Why must we have a bluestocking for a daughter?"

Sarah blinked rapidly, doing her best to push her tears back. She had been sitting in her favorite place in the house – in the library – engrossed in a book on the latest discoveries of certain birds on the continent only for her mother and father to come into the room. No doubt they had been looking for her but, given that she was seated in the window seat with the curtain drawn so as to hide her away all the more, they did not know her to be present.

"She is very plain, my dear." Lady Harcastle replied, making Sarah's eyes squeeze shut such was the pain now rifling through her. "And she is the youngest of our five, so there has been some neglect there on my part."

Lord Harcastle sighed so heavily, it seemed to fill the room. "All the same, my dear, there must be something we can do. I cannot accept – I *will* not accept – that one of my children remains unwed."

"I do not want a spinster for a daughter as much as you," came the reply, "but we have permitted her to read as freely as she wishes for a very long time. I confess that I did not ever think her to be a bluestocking, presuming only that she read either foolish novels or of matters pertaining to a lady's etiquette, but now I learn that she is well versed in all manner of things! Last evening's dinner was a complete embarrassment for us all."

Sarah closed her eyes tightly, putting one hand to her mouth. Last evening, her father had brought a gentleman by the name of Lord Johnston to their estate for dinner. He had apparently become acquainted with the fellow some months ago on a business matter and Sarah had thought nothing of it, until she saw her mother's sharp glances towards her, the nods of the head in the direction of the gentleman and the occasional widening of the eyes when Sarah had said something that was, by her mother's standards, entirely unnecessary. Slowly, she had come to understand that her parents had hoped for a match to be made between them, that there would be an interest in her on the part of the gentleman but, evidently, her conversation had put an end to those hopes. Sarah had not thought there was anything wrong in what she had spoken of, sharing her thoughts on various matters of present considerations within society and out of it, speaking of her interest in all matters as regarded animals and the newly discovered species abroad… but evidently, this had turned Lord Johnston away from her.

"Will you take her to London this Season, as you had thought?" Lord Harcastle's voice was low, filled with concern. "My dear, she could bring all the more embarrassment to us if she speaks as she did last evening. Perhaps it would be better if I made an arrangement, found someone who would be willing to marry her despite her bluestocking tendencies."

No, please! Sarah's heart began to pound, waiting for judgement to fall. Her mother would either agree to do as he had suggested or would agree to take Sarah to London for the Season – her second Season – as had been previously stated. The silence was overpowering her, bringing great fear to her heart as she waited, her body beginning to tremble. As the youngest of four daughters and one son, Sarah had been waiting for her time to make her presence known amongst society and was yet to be given that moment. Yes, she had made her debut last Season but her elder sister, Martha, had been also seeking a match and her engagement to Lord Thurstwick had overshadowed Sarah's Season. She had spent more time reading and being in her own company than she had been in society, having been somewhat neglected by her mother who had done all she could to make sure that Martha's match had been made certain. Sarah had told herself repeatedly that she did not mind such a thing, that it was important for Martha to have a secure future and that her time would come... though now, it seemed, it might still be snatched from her.

"I will speak with her." Lady Harcastle sounded almost sorrowful, as though Sarah's interest in expanding her mind was a great source of pain. "I will make it clear that this reading, this constant thought of pursuing yet more knowledge must come to an end. If she agrees, then I will take her to London and the Season will commence. If she does not, then we will simply find her a match."

"A wise consideration, my dear." Lord Harcastle cleared his throat gently. "I am aware that Lord Whitefield is looking for a bride."

Shock ricocheted around Sarah's heart, making her gasp for air. Lord Whitefield was a gentleman close to her father in age, known for his dark moods, ill temper and general unkind disposition. Surely they would not do such a thing as marry her to that fellow! Sarah well understood that her parents wished for all of their children to marry but they would not really marry her to a gentleman such as Lord Whitefield merely to make certain what *they* intended came to pass, would they?

"That could be a potential match, yes."

Sarah shuddered. *Yes, they would.*

"I will speak to her first before any decision is made, however," her mother continued, as Lord Harcastle harrumphed, clearly relieved that some sort of decision had been made. "Though we must find her first!"

They soon quit the room to go in search of her and, the

moment the door closed behind them, Sarah let out a sob that she had been fighting to hold back. The door to her emotions was loosened and she broke down completely, burying her face in her hands as she cried.

How injurious her parents had been to her! To believe that her desire to read more, to learn all she could was something to be ashamed about, to call it a mortification made Sarah's heart cry out with sorrow. And this was to be taken away from her if she was to go back to society? If she was to have her Season, then she would have to give up that thing that she loved the most – her books. Could she do it? Could she promise she would not read any longer? Pretend that she was not as learned as she truly was simply so that a gentleman's ego would not be damaged in any way? Sarah wiped her eyes, feeling herself more sorrowful.

What else is there to induce a gentleman's interest? she asked herself, her heart tearing. *I am a bluestocking, it seems, and have not even beautiful features to attract anyone to me.* Yes, she knew that she was not the most beautiful of the sisters but to have been called plain made her feel as though she was not even worth looking at.

But if I refuse to give up my reading, then I will be forced to marry Lord Whitefield.

The thought of such a thing made her shudder violently as she put her head back and rested it against the wall behind her. Tears still came to her eyes but they were not as fervent as before. Swallowing hard, she took in a deep breath.

I will not give up my books, she told herself, firmly. *But mayhap I will not have to. I have overheard my parents speaking, I know what it is that they are going to demand from me and I can agree to it while refusing to do what it is that they ask.* She took in another breath, feeling herself a little more at ease. *I will pretend to give it all up while keeping all that I love close to my heart,* she told herself, firmly. *Somehow, I will find a way. I must.*

Chapter One

"Sarah? I wish to speak with you before we step out into society."

Sarah, who had only just finished her preparations for her first ball of the Season, turned to look back at her mother. "Good evening, Mama," she said, calmly, all too aware of what this conversation was to be. "I am quite ready, as you see. We shall not be tardy, if that is your concern."

"No, that is not my concern," her mother answered, a little sharply. "My goodness, Sarah, is that what you are to wear about your neck? Do you not think that a string of pearls might do better than a single diamond pendant?"

Sarah kept her chin lifted and her gaze steady, aware of her mother's seeming need to be critical of something, regardless of what it was. "I am contented with this, Mama."

Her mother clicked her tongue in disapproval. "No, I think the pearls will do much better. Here, now, go and fetch the pearls and replace this pendant at once."

Sarah turned to her maid. "No, the pendant will do quite well," she said, speaking over her mother's order. "You can retire now."

Lady Harcastle threw up her hands as the maid glanced from one to the other, clearly uncertain as to whom she ought to listen to. "Whatever is the matter with you, Sarah? I am doing my best for you and —"

"I am still able to make my own choices, Mama," Sarah answered, aware that she had interrupted but continuing on regardless. "I have already given up a great deal, though you may not think it. I should like to have a modicum of independence, if I can."

Lady Harcastle sighed, shook her head and then

dismissed the maid with a wave of her hand. "Very well. Now, the reason I have come to speak with you is as regards your conduct this evening."

Sarah said nothing but merely lifted an eyebrow.

"You are *not* to speak of anything that a young lady would not know of otherwise. I am well aware that you have done a good deal of reading of late and that you consider yourself a little more learned than the other young ladies but that is not something that you are to promote. Indeed, no-one else is to know of it, particularly not the gentlemen that you are in company with. Do I make myself clear?"

"Yes, Mama." The desire to argue, to throw back a harsh response to her mother's demands grew heavy on Sarah's tongue but she kept it back with an effort. There would be little point in arguing. After what she had overheard that day in the library, Sarah had decided to simply agree to all that her parents asked of her – to a point, of course – while, at the same time, disobeying them completely. The books that her mother had demanded she give up had all been left at the Harcastle estate but Sarah had every intention of getting her hands on yet more books where she could. It was unfortunate that her mother had insisted on having the library here at the London townhouse locked but it had not deterred Sarah in the least. Somehow, she would find a way back to her passion for learning regardless of what her mother or father knew.

"If a gentleman asks you what interest you have, what shall you say?"

I shall tell them that I have found the nesting habits of various seabirds to be of great interest of late, Sarah thought to herself, her lips twitching as she dropped her gaze. "I enjoy painting and playing the pianoforte. I do not enjoy embroidery, though I suppose I am meant to, being a young lady of quality." She lifted her gaze back to her mother, seeing the slight narrowing of Lady Harcastle's eyes. Clearly, her mother was uncertain as to whether or not Sarah was entirely serious in this.

"You can refrain from the latter," her mother said firmly, clearly making certain that Sarah understood her entirely. "I do not understand why you think to jest with me when there is clearly so much at stake here! You have much to do and much to gain, might I remind you? This is your only chance to –"

"My only chance to gain a husband, yes, I know," Sarah interrupted, now a little more frustrated with her mother's sharp words and hard manner. "You have made this all very clear to me, Mama, and I fully understand what it is you expect."

Her mother's gaze grew a little more icy. "And do you understand what will happen if you determine to go against what your father and I have dictated? What will happen if you stray from the agreements you have made?"

Sarah held her mother's gaze without blinking, her heart beating a little more quickly as she spoke the words she knew her mother wanted to hear but which she herself did not really mean. "Mama, I know that I must not speak of my learning, I must not talk about my love of reading and must not seek out any books with which to continue on with my passion. I understand that the gentlemen of London must not have even the smallest awareness that I am a bluestocking, they must not know that I have an interest in such things and I am to hide my character completely. Instead, I must alter myself so that I am nothing more than I ought to be. I will be the entirely proper young lady who must speak only of the pianoforte, of her interest in painting and nothing more. As well as this, I must speak to the gentlemen of *their* desires, hearing of *their* interests rather than my own and must never fall into any sort of discussion with any of the gentlemen I become acquainted with. My main responsibility is only to listen to the gentlemen I speak to, in the hope that by doing so, they will find me all that they expect of a young lady."

The edge of her mother's lip curled for a moment but then flattened again, making Sarah aware that her mother was uncertain as to how to respond. Either she was unsure as to whether or not Sarah was speaking the truth in genuine acceptance or if she was speaking with a hint of irony.

Sarah did not give her more time to consider. "Shall we depart, Mama? We will be tardy otherwise and I know you will not wish to be so. It would make a very bad impression."

"Yes, I suppose it would," came the reply, as her mother, with another sharp look, finally turned towards the door. "And do not put a foot – or even a word – wrong, Sarah. You are to be a bluestocking no longer."

***

"Good evening, Lady Sarah."

Sarah chuckled as she inclined her head, smiling at her friend. "My dear Catherine, I do not think that you need to call me Lady Sarah, since last Season we were not referring to each other in such a way!"

Lady Catherine immediately smiled, her eyes warm. "I am glad to hear it! I wanted to be cautious, since it has been some time since we were in one another's company."

Sarah sighed and, turning, began to walk alongside Lady Catherine as they both dutifully followed after their mothers. "Indeed it has. I have been residing at home and did not come to London for even the little Season, much to my chagrin. My mother declared that she was quite worn out after Martha's wedding and thus, we had to rest for some months."

Lady Catherine's eyebrows lifted at Sarah's tone, and Sarah offered her a wry smile.

"You know very well that it was not because of the gentlemen here in London that I thought to escape," she laughed as Lady Catherine grinned. "You know, I am sure, that I wanted nothing more than to get to the bookshops and to the great London Library."

"Indeed, I was certain that was what you were thinking of," came the reply. "But you will be glad to be in London again now, yes?"

At this, Sarah's stomach twisted and she shook her head. "I am afraid not. My mother and father have only recently discovered my love of reading and the great learning which has come with it and, subsequently, they have decided that they are mortified to hear of such a thing and have demanded that I do not pick up another book during my time here in London... if ever again!"

"Truly?" Lady Catherine's eyes were wide with astonishment. "Why ever should they say such a thing?"

Recalling what she had overheard, Sarah dropped her gaze, a knot in her throat which still came to her every time she considered it. "I believe their words were that they did not want to have a bluestocking for a daughter. No gentleman will ever consider me, they have said, so thus, I must come to London and pretend that I am vapid and even a little insipid so as to gain what they think is the most profitable." The words were like ash on her tongue and she scowled as she spoke, feeling the kick of pain in her heart all over again.

"That is astonishing!" Lady Catherine exclaimed. "Surely you have not agreed to it?"

Sarah looked back at her friend. "If I had not, then my father would have arranged a match for me. That might not have been a particularly bad outcome, were it not for the fact that the gentleman he was considering was dreadful, both in terms of his age and his character."

Lady Catherine caught her breath and Sarah nodded slowly, confirming that this was true.

"It was a true threat, though I was not meant to have overheard it," she explained, quickly. "Therefore, I resolved that I would accept what my mother put to me and I would give up my books and my learning… while still refusing to give up my books and my learning."

Her friend frowned. "And how are you to go about that?"

"Very carefully," Sarah answered, with a small smile. "I hoped that, mayhap, our friendship might be one of the ways in which I can continue on in my reading?"

"Of course!" Lady Catherine exclaimed. "We could walk in town together and I could *insist* upon stepping into a bookshop and you, given your kindness, would have no choice but to come with me. Thereafter, if you found a book which you wished to purchase, I could keep it with me and when you come to take tea, for example, you could spend some time reading it there."

A sense of relief settled upon Sarah immediately. "Precisely what I was hoping for," she said, seeing her friend's eyes light up. "I do appreciate you, Catherine. You and I share an interest in reading and I am grateful for your support in this."

"I am horrified that you have been forced into this, I must say," Lady Catherine answered, slipping one arm through Sarah's. "What will you do as regards the gentlemen of London? Will you truly pretend to be nothing more than a foolish young lady who knows very little aside from how to embroider and which fashion plate is the most popular?"

Sarah winced. "I do not know what I shall do," she said, honestly. "I had not really considered that, as yet. I must do what my mother has stated, of course, for the consequences of refusing would be severe but at the same time, I cannot imagine what it would be like to either be courted by or even married to a gentleman who did not truly know who I was! That is what my mother wishes for me to do and my own heart has turned away from that idea in the strongest manner – but what else is there for me to do?"

Her friend's lips pulled to one side as she thought and Sarah waited hopefully, eager to hear what wisdom it was Lady Catherine had to offer. She had spent the past few weeks fretting over her mother's insistence that she must marry, fully aware that she could not feign frivolity throughout her Season, courtship, and eventually, her married life. However, what other option did she have? She could not disobey her mother for fear of what consequences would follow but neither could she pretend to any gentleman truly interested in her that she was unintelligent and did not vastly enjoy delving into books!

Her hopes were dashed as Lady Catherine shook her head and sighed.

"I cannot offer you any advice, I am afraid," she answered as Sarah's shoulders dropped a little. "It is a very difficult situation, I must say."

"It is," Sarah agreed, heavily, "and I do not know how I am to escape from it. I – oh!"

This exclamation came from her lips as something heavy fell on her foot, followed by a figure knocking back into her. With another cry, Sarah fell back, caught by Lady Catherine who then held onto her tightly, helping her not to collapse to the floor.

"Whatever are you doing?"

A dark, angry voice rang around Sarah's mind as she fought to try and regain her composure. Her foot was aching, embarrassment burning through her as she tried to stand but found she could not.

"What did you do, Sarah?"

Sarah tried to answer her mother who had rounded on her as though this was her doing but she could not, such was the intensity of the pain which was now creeping up her leg.

"Sarah did nothing wrong! It was *this* oaf who barreled into her and caused her some injury of some sort." Lady Catherine was immediately at Sarah's defense, speaking boldly despite being surrounded by a great crowd of gentlemen and ladies, many of whom started to show an interest in what was going on.

"It is nothing," Sarah tried to say, though this was followed by another exclamation as she tried to set her foot down on the floor.

"Good gracious!" Her mother, now perhaps realizing Sarah was not at fault and was, in fact, truly injured, came to clasp Sarah's other arm so that she was supported on both sides. "Might I ask what it is you think you are doing in injuring my daughter in this manner?"

The gentleman scowled, his dark green eyes narrowed, a shock of fair hair falling over his forehead. "I did nothing to injure your daughter, ma'am. It was her own foolish fault, getting in my way as she did."

"*You* stepped back without looking where you were going or what you were doing!" Lady Catherine cried as Sarah, still struggling with the pain, managed to nod. "In doing so, you have clearly stepped very heavily back upon this lady's foot and have injured her to the point that she is unable to stand."

"It is just as Lady Catherine says."

Sarah turned her gaze to another young lady, seeing her narrow her eyes at the gentleman.

"Both my mother and I were witness to it," she continued, as the lady next to her – the one Sarah presumed to be the lady's mother – nodded. "This young lady – "

"Lady Sarah, daughter to the Earl of Harcastle," Sarah's mother put in, as the young lady continued.

"This young lady, Lady Sarah, was injured solely because of your inconsideration and foolishness."

"And then you have the audacity to attempt to blame her for it?" the older lady added, her voice filled with an authority which appeared to set the gentleman back given the way the scowl began to lift from his face. "She did nothing wrong! All she was doing was walking through the ballroom with her friend and *you* were the one who behaved with idiocy and thoughtlessness. Might I suggest that you take a moment and, thereafter, apologise? Mayhap you might also assist the young lady to a chair? It is clear that your heavy foot has caused her to be unable to even walk at this moment!"

Sarah closed her eyes, her face suffused with heat. "I – I am sure that I do not need any assistance though I am grateful for your concern." She tried then to put her foot down, only to stifle yet another cry as more pain shot through her ankle.

"You see?" her mother cried, only for the gentleman to step forward.

"Of course. Permit me, if you please."

Before Sarah could protest, before she could even say a single word, the gentleman had swept her up in his arms and, with her skirts draped over his arm, he carried her bodily to the back of the ballroom. She dared not look at him, however, finding herself utterly mortified that she was being treated in such a way – and that he felt the need to do so.

"I did not mean to hurt you," he muttered, his great strides eating up the floor as gentlemen and ladies stepped out of their way, astonishment written on every face. "Might I enquire as to your name?"

Sarah forced herself to glance at him. "Did you not hear it?"

The gentleman shook his head, his fair hair sweeping close to his eyes, his square jaw set and rather tight.

"Oh." Seeing now that he was doing this so that he would not be berated by anyone or bring any stain upon his reputation, Sarah swallowed tightly. "Lady Sarah. Daughter to the Earl of Harcastle."

"I see." He waited for a moment as the footmen opened the door that led out to the hallway. "A private parlour, if you please. The lady has injured herself."

The footman nodded and led him forward and the gentleman continued on effortlessly, as though she weighed very little.

"Might... might I ask as to your name?"

The gentleman glanced at her but there was no warmth in his eyes. Instead, there was a flicker in his eyes which spoke of irritation, perhaps of anger and Sarah shrank back within herself.

"The Marquess of Downfield," he stated, though he quickly looked away from her again. "Here now. Let me set you down upon this couch and then I shall send the footmen to assist you."

Sarah was a little surprised at how gently the gentleman let her rest on the couch, though as he set her down, the scent of cinnamon and sweet pine brushed across her senses, making her stomach kick suddenly. She looked away, smoothing her skirts as quickly as she could though her mother was present beside her in a moment.

"I will take the situation in hand from here," Lady Harcastle stated, barely glancing at the gentleman. "Thank you for your assistance, though I do hope you will be a good deal more cautious in the future."

Closing her eyes briefly – though silently reminding herself that she did not need to feel any sort of embarrassment given that the gentleman *was* responsible for what had taken place – Sarah heard him cough quietly as though to rid himself of whatever his first response was to have been.

"But of course. Do excuse me."

He left then without another word, leaving Sarah, her mother and a concerned looking Lady Catherine together in the room.

"Mama has gone to send a footman for the doctor," Lady Catherine told her, turning her head to glance after the gentleman though he quit the room without so much as a backwards look towards her. "I do hope that he apologised profusely to you for what he did and for the blame which he then tried to place upon you?"

"I – " Sarah stopped dead, frowning as she realized that the gentleman had not said a single word of apology to her. "Now that I think of it, I do not think that he did."

"What arrogance!" Lady Harcastle exclaimed, coming to pull a small stool forward so that Sarah could turn and set her injured ankle upon it. "I would have thought that any decent gentleman might have apologised for such an action."

"He did say that he had not meant to hurt me."

"But that is no apology!" her mother exclaimed, as

Lady Catherine nodded fervently. "It is a dreadful thing he has done for now you shall not be able to dance or perhaps even walk for a time! You will not be able to attend balls or soirees and will have to rest at home, I am sure of it!"

Sarah blinked, letting her gaze turn to Lady Catherine who, after a moment, let her lips twitch. "That is a great pity, Mama," Sarah murmured, now aware that Lady Catherine knew precisely what she was thinking. "But I am sure that in time, I will recover."

"I will call upon you very often in that time," Lady Catherine promised, a slight gleam in her eye. "Tomorrow, certainly! I will bring you some things to cheer your spirits as you wait to recover."

"I thank you," Sarah answered, wincing as her foot was stretched out carefully by her mother so that it now rested on the stool. All the same, she considered, despite the pain in her ankle, there was now the sudden hope that she would be given the chance to read and that Lady Catherine would provide her with the means to do so. Perhaps this gentleman, despite his foolishness, had given her some happiness for if she could read again, even for a time, then that was a most excellent thing!

Chapter Two

Foolish girl.

Matthew flicked one hand towards the footman standing nearby. "Another."

The footman obliged at once, stepping away to fetch a second brandy, though Matthew was quickly joined by not one but three of his grinning friends.

"Lord Dover, Lord Stephenson?" Matthew narrowed his eyes in jest as he looked to his third – and closest – friend. "Lord Rutherford. Is there something that I can do for you all?"

"You did leave the ball rather quickly," Lord Stephenson said, as the other two nodded. "We presumed that you must be a little ill at ease after what happened and we thought to come and make certain that all was quite well."

"Given that I have only come to the card room, I hardly think that this could be considered *leaving* the ball."

"You have not come back to our conversation, however," Lord Dover put in. "Nor have you sought to dance with anyone. That is considered leaving, I think?"

Lord Rutherford threw up his hands. "It was an accident, old boy! You need not step away from the joviality of the ball – and all the very fine ladies who wish for your company – because of one young lady."

Matthew scowled. "I did not appreciate being berated in front of the other guests."

His friends all glanced at each other and Matthew's scowl deepened.

"You think that I brought that upon myself, I suppose," he grated. "I am sure that the lady in question was quite foolish, that she knocked into me or some such thing. Thereafter, I lost my footing and that is why she is injured."

"No doubt," Lord Stephenson said, in a tone which told Matthew that he did not believe him. "But all the same, you did as was told of you and though that must have been a little frustrating, it is done and the lady is being cared for."

"I did not apologise," Matthew told him, seeing Lord Rutherford's eyebrows lift. "I made certain to say that I did not mean to injure her and –"

"Then you shall have to call tomorrow."

Matthew blinked, his eyebrows now falling low over his eyes. "I beg your pardon?"

James, the Earl of Rutherford, had been Matthew's friend for as long as Matthew could remember. They had played together as children, had gone to Eton together and he could always rely on him in every situation. He was also known for being rather blunt, for speaking just as he saw things and though it was a quality that Matthew appreciated, it was, mayhap, not something that he wished to hear at the present moment.

It appeared he was going to be given Lord Rutherford's thoughts regardless, however.

"You wish to blame the lady and whether you are determined to believe yourself quite without fault, you must still, as a gentleman, go to apologise. It is expected and you should certainly do such a thing, if you do not want your reputation to be damaged."

Lord Dover and Lord Stephenson glanced at each other but said nothing, leaving Matthew's frustration to grow. Evidently, they agreed with Lord Rutherford, else they would have said outright. It seemed that he was outnumbered.

"I have no desire to go and speak with the lady," he grumbled, recalling how he had pulled her into his arms and seen her hazel eyes widen in shock, her face white. He had felt not a single iota of sympathy nor of desire. "It will be a waste of my time and I have already made plans to go and call upon a few various young ladies of society."

Lord Dover snorted. "No doubt to try and ascertain their interest in *you* rather than having any real interest in them themselves, yes?"

Matthew shrugged, having no inclination to hide such a thing from his friends given that they all knew him so well. "I am already interested to know which young ladies hope for more of my attentions. That does not mean that I am eager to give them, of course! It is only because I find myself... drawn to that notion."

Lord Stephenson rolled his eyes. "You simply like knowing that there are many young ladies – and older ladies – in London who are *desperate* for your attentions. It pleases you to know that when you walk into a ballroom, a good many eyes are resting upon you. Is that not so?"

Considering this for a moment – and taking no offence at it – Matthew shrugged for the second time and then let himself smile. "That may be the truth but I shall not properly admit to it." Silently, he acknowledged that everything Lord Stephenson had said was quite true but he would certainly never admit to it. Yes, it *did* fill him with delight to know that there were so many young ladies who admired him and sought his interest, what was so troublesome about that?

"It will not take you long to call upon the lady and apologise," Lord Rutherford told him, bringing the subject back to the young lady. "What was her name, now? I might be acquainted with her."

"Lady Sarah." Matthew saw his friend nod slowly. "Her father is the Earl of Harcastle."

Lord Rutherford's expression cleared. "Ah yes, of

course. That gentleman is *very* wealthy and very influential indeed, I must say. He has a strong mind when it comes to business and I know that many a gentleman has gone to him for advice. It would be wise of you not to set yourself against such a gentleman."

Matthew snorted. "I have more than enough wealth to keep me satisfied."

"Be that as it may, it is your reputation I am concerned about. If Lord Harcastle tells anyone that he thinks poorly of you, then I can assure you that society will no longer take such a favorable look." Lord Rutherford tilted his head and arched one eyebrow. "And as you have just said, you do enjoy being admired."

"I did not say that... precisely," Matthew said, somewhat fiercely, though the way his friend grinned took away some of his irritation. "Very well, if I must then I shall go and speak with Lady Sarah and apologise. Tomorrow, of course."

"And bring flowers," Lord Dover added, as Lord Rutherford nodded. "That will show that you truly are contrite, even if you are not."

"Flowers?" Matthew grimaced. "I have not brought flowers to a lady in many a month. I believe that the last time I did so, it was to my mother!"

This made all his friends laugh, though that had not been Matthew's intention.

"All the more reason for you to do so. It will be good for you to show consideration in that marked way," Lord Rutherford told him. "And why do you not *tell* the young lady that it has been so long since you brought flowers to someone? That will make her feel all the more that you are truly apologetic, I am sure."

Seeing that there was now no way for him to escape

this, no way for him to choose *not* to do as his friends suggested, Matthew let out a long, pronounced sigh but no one made any other remark, no-one expressed sympathy or the like to him. Instead, they began talking of something else, speaking of which young lady they were to dance with next and Matthew slowly sank down in his chair, his expression still dark and his frustration very much present.

There was to be nothing for it, however. He would have no other choice but to call upon Lady Sarah and express his apologies profusely, even though he would not be speaking a single, genuine word. He would have to do it, however, and perhaps then, Matthew considered, he would be able to return to society and all that he enjoyed without giving the lady a further thought.

***

"Good afternoon, Lady Sarah. I have come to see how you fare this afternoon." Matthew bowed his head, aware of the ball of impatience which was, at present, rattling around within him. He did not want to be here. He did not want to spend time in this young lady's company, having no interest in her whatsoever and yet, here he was, bowing and smiling and holding out the bouquet of roses he had purchased for her. "I do hope that my foolishness last evening has not caused you too great a pain?"

Lady Sarah gestured to the maid to take the roses from him, her chestnut curls swinging gently from where they had been pulled to the back of her head. Then she turned her gaze to him, steady as she watched him though as yet, she had not said a single word.

Matthew cleared his throat, his hands clasped behind his back. "I – I suppose that I must also apologise for my behaviour last evening. I was not considerate nor was I careful and I am mortified that you were brought to such pain."

"It is good to hear that there is some contrition, at least."

Matthew turned his head, just to see the lady of the house walk into the room, her eyes flashing with evident anger as he bowed to her.

"I confess that I was greatly upset, not only that you injured my daughter but that, thereafter, you did not think to apologise," Lady Harcastle said, folding her arms over her chest as her eyes narrowed. "I am appreciative that you carried my daughter to a place where she might rest but I do believe that not even a single word of apology was spoken to her? That is something of a disgrace and – "

"Mama, Lord Downfield has come now to apologise." Lady Sarah spoke with a firmness to her tone, her words clear and her gaze now fixed to her mother. "I do not think that we need to berate him now."

Lady Harcastle sniffed and then looked away. "All the same, I – "

"Might we fetch a tea tray?" Lady Sarah gestured to Matthew, her eyes now turning to him rather than to her mother. "You will stay for a few minutes, I hope? We can make certain that there is no lingering tension, no uncertain feeling between us any longer and all will be well." Her eyes widened just a fraction, followed by a very swift glance towards her mother and, despite himself, Matthew smiled. The lady was clearly attempting to make it plain to him that her own mother would not be satisfied with a mere apology from him, from only a few minutes standing on her floor. If he wanted to be done with the matter, if he wished for his life to return to the same happiness and freedom as he had been enjoying these last few weeks, then he would be required to take tea and to sit with Lady Sarah and Lady Harcastle for a time.

But there is still Lady Sophia whom I wish to call upon, he reminded himself, clearing his throat as he looked away. *And Lady Bettina who is expecting me also.*

"A few minutes, of course." Begrudgingly, he sat down in a chair indicated to him by Lady Harcastle. "I am truly sorry for what took place, Lady Sarah. I should have taken more care."

"And you should not have blamed my daughter for your own foolishness."

Matthew hid his grimace with an effort but nodded. "You are quite correct there also, Lady Harcastle. I should not have placed any sort of blame on your daughter. It was entirely my own doing and I am very sorry indeed for the pain which has been caused."

"It is quite all right. I understand that these things can happen, especially when there is a great crush." Lady Sarah offered him a small smile though her eyes did not linger on his for more than a brief moment. "Ah, here is the tea now."

"*I* will pour it, since you cannot," Lady Harcastle said, the emphasis making Matthew wince. "The doctor says that my daughter will have to rest for a fortnight, Lord Downfield. Two weeks! Two weeks that she shall be out of society!"

Lady Sarah coughed quietly. "That is not quite correct, Mama," she said, as Lady Harcastle rose to pour the tea. "I am to stay resting for a sennight but thereafter, can attend soirees and balls, just so long as I do not dance or spend too long on my feet."

Lady Harcastle sniffed. "All the same, it is most inconvenient and dreadfully unfair to a young lady such as yourself who is *looking* for a match this Season. You have truly done her a disservice by your actions, Lord Downfield. I do hope you realise the extent of it."

Matthew opened his mouth to speak, only to close it again. Every moment here was agony, his words burning on his lips as he forced them back, determined that he would not speak defensively given that it would, no doubt, cause all the more difficulty for him. It was best simply to endure, he told himself, so that he would not find himself berated all the more.

"Are you in London for the Season, Lord Downfield?" Lady Sarah's voice was gentle enough but she was still refusing to look at him for any more than a brief moment and for whatever reason, that displeased him.

"Yes, I am. I have been in London for a good many Seasons and I have not tired of them as yet." That much was true, for Matthew had attended the Season just as soon as he had been able and given that he did not have to make a debut as the young ladies of London did, it had been at a somewhat young age when he had first stepped into society. "I took on the title at only three years ago, however," he clarified, seeing Lady Harcastle's brows furrow, "but I was in London for a good many years before that, you understand."

"And you have still not taken a bride?" Lady Harcastle asked, making Lady Sarah drop her head, her cheeks turning a bright shade of red. "That is a little surprising, is it not? I would have thought that a gentleman with your standing and your title would have been eager to produce the heir."

"Mama," Lady Sarah breathed but Lady Harcastle only shrugged, clearly not in the least bit concerned about what it was that either Sarah or Matthew himself thought of her bold question.

"It is not yet the right time," Matthew answered, stiffly. "For the moment, Lady Harcastle, I am quite contented to attend London and enjoy myself there, with my acquaintances and close friends. It makes for an excellent few months and, given what has been a rather difficult year as regards some of my business matters, it is a good respite."

Lady Harcastle's eyebrows lifted but Matthew rose quickly to his feet, having barely taken even a sip of his tea.

"And I shall take my leave of you now, so that you do not become wearied by my presence," he said, bowing quickly. "Do excuse me, Lady Sarah, Lady Harcastle. I pray, once again, that you would accept my apologies for what happened last evening and for the suffering that you are going through. Good afternoon."

"I do expect you to call again, Lord Downfield?"

Matthew stopped, turning to see Lady Harcastle now on her feet, her hands at her hips and her eyes sharp as she lifted her chin just a notch.

"You *will* call again, will you not?"

Despite this being a question, Matthew heard it more as a statement – one that he had no choice but to agree to. He could refuse, of course, he could say that he had no intention of coming back to call upon her again but then, in doing so, he would risk the wrath of Lord Downfield who might wish to tell others about his refusal.

"Indeed, I shall," he muttered, inclining his head towards the lady who was now looking back at him with rather wide eyes, her hands in her lap though Matthew could see the shock of his words twisting through her expression. "I will call again very soon. Good afternoon, Lady Harcastle." He bowed and, with relief crashing over him, stepped out of the room and quickly made his way back along to the front of the house.

The sooner she recovers, the better it shall be for me this Season, he told himself as the door was opened for him and he stepped outside. *Goodness, what a dreadful situation! Once I am free of her, I shall return to my happy situation and forget all about Lady Sarah and her injury. That shall be a sweet relief indeed!*

Chapter Three

"Are you alone?"

Sarah nodded fervently as Lady Catherine came into the room, her eyes sparking. "I am. Did you bring me something?"

Lady Catherine nodded, holding out a parcel to her. "I have found an excellent book on the history of France. I know that you do enjoy reading about the natural world but –"

"I am delighted with it, thank you." Sarah reached out and unwrapped the book from its brown paper, her heart spinning with delight as she finally held the book in her hands. "I have missed reading a great deal, I confess. How good it is now to have something here to feed my mind!"

"It must have been very difficult these last few days to sit at home without company and without books," Lady Catherine replied, as Sarah nodded. "How long is it until you can step back into society."

Sarah sighed. "I have told my mother that I can make my way from room to room already without too much pain, although I do limp a great deal, but she is insisting that I do as the doctor said and wait at home for the sennight. Thereafter, I shall be able to return to society but I will not be able to dance." She laughed softly at her friend's concerned expression. "I do not mind that a great deal. Dancing has never been a passion of mine, I confess."

"That is no great concern, then." Lady Catherine's expression cleared and she smiled. "And has Lord Downfield come to call upon you again?"

"He has not," Sarah replied with a shrug, "though I cannot say that I am disappointed. He is a most displeasing gentleman, I think."

Her friend grimaced. "Indeed! I have been speaking to a few of our acquaintances in society and they all say that while Lord Downfield is an often sought out gentleman, with a high title, a good deal of wealth and an amiable character, he is still very arrogant indeed."

"And inconsiderate with it," Sarah added, scowling as she recalled how he had tried to force the blame upon *her* for what had happened. "He did come to call, at least, though I am sure that it was only because he was forced to do so by the expectation of society. He showed no genuine interest in me, his apology – though appreciated – came from a gentleman who had no real desire to do so. No doubt it was all done to make certain that his reputation was kept quite pristine, particularly after what he did. I was glad that there were those – including yourself – who came to my defense. I am quite sure he would have continued on, determined to place the blame upon me rather than taking responsibility upon himself."

"I quite agree." Lady Catherine sighed and shook her head. "At least now we know that he is *not* a gentleman to seek out the company of."

Sarah was about to agree, only for the maid to come to the door. She bobbed a curtsy then came in to hand Sarah a calling card, making Sarah's eyes widen.

"Lord Downfield has come to call!" she whispered, as Lady Catherine's eyes flared. "You will stay with me, yes? I know that my mother is present in the house but she was very severe indeed with him the last time he called – not that he did not deserve it, of course – but it did make for a rather tense cup of tea."

"Of course I will stay." A glimmer of a smile touched Lady Catherine's lips. "Mayhap *I* shall be the severe one this time rather than your mother!"

A laugh escaped from Sarah's lips – though it was, she recognized, holding a good deal of anxiety also – as she indicated to the maid to bring the gentleman in. She herself did not rise to her feet, even though her ankle was no longer resting on a small stool and she could have very easily done so. Part of her wanted him to see her still injured, wanted to see that his foolishness meant her pain still lingered. Whether it was his actions or his arrogance that irritated her, she did not know, but she remained seated regardless.

"Good afternoon, Lady Sarah." Lord Downfield bowed, then looked towards Lady Catherine. "And good afternoon to you also."

"Lady Catherine." Sarah gestured to her friend. "Mayhap you have not yet been introduced? This is my very dear friend, Lady Catherine. Her father is the Earl of Newly."

"I see." The gentleman bowed again but there was no smile on his face, no sense of delight in his expression. "I came to see how you were, Lady Sarah but it appears that you have recovered well already!"

Surprise had Sarah's eyebrows lifting as she looked to Lady Catherine for a moment. "And might I ask how you surmise that?"

"Your foot is no longer held out," he told her, clasping his hands behind his back, accentuating his broad shoulders and, for a moment, Sarah quite lost herself as she took him in. Despite his egotism, she had to admit that he was a handsome gentleman, even though his expression always appeared to be tight with either irritation or anger. *Though that may well only be in my company, given what has happened between us.*

"My *dear* friend can do nothing without assistance!" Lady Catherine exclaimed, making Lord Downfield jump given how loud her voice had become in a single instant. "She can stand, yes, but she must have aid to walk anywhere and there is still a great deal of pain surrounding her ankle. How very bold of you to make such a statement based on only what you can see, Lord Downfield! I would have thought that a gentleman such as yourself would have had the consideration to *ask* a young lady how she fared instead of making such a sweeping judgement."

Sarah hid a smile, seeing now that Lady Catherine had been quite determined in her desire to be just as sharp as Lady Harcastle had been. Lord Downfield, however, did not look in the least bit pleased. Instead, he scowled, dropped his hands to his sides and looked away.

"Might I ask how you are, Lady Sarah?" he muttered, passing one hand over his eyes as though he could not bring himself to look at her. "I am sorry to hear that you are still in pain."

Hesitating for a moment, Sarah chose to be truthful rather than to pretend otherwise. "My ankle is healing well," she said, as the gentleman finally brought his gaze to hers. "There is still lingering pain and I certainly do require a shoulder to lean on when I walk but I hope to join society again very soon... though I shall have to do a good deal of sitting down and resting initially. Thank you for your concern."

The Marquess sniffed, lifted his chin and then offered a small, tight smile. "That is good. I do hope to see you again in society. Excuse me."

Sarah blinked in surprise as the gentleman turned, clearly ready to take his leave. Astonished, she looked then to Lady Catherine, who was now frowning heavily.

"That is all you wish to say?" Lady Catherine asked, halting Lord Downfield as he approached the door. "You come here, speak rather bluntly to Lady Sarah and then intend to take your leave? And you do this after coming here empty handed?"

Lord Downfield turned on his heel, his jaw jutting forward. "Mayhap your friend has not informed you of this, but I did bring flowers the last time I attended Lady Sarah."

"Yes, he did," Sarah answered, quickly, seeing that Lady Catherine was doing all she could to make the gentleman feel a little guilty for what he had done but thinking now that she had done quite enough. Lord Downfield was clearly an arrogant sort and no matter what was said or how many things were thrown to him, he was not about to change. She would not have a genuine apology from him, would not have a true or sincere concern over her injury. There was very little point in continuing on with their acquaintance, given how fraught it was already. "I did not expect anything more, Lady Catherine, I assure you."

Her friend shot her a look and Sarah widened her eyes, just a little, hoping that she understood.

"Still, I would have expected more from a gentleman." Lady Catherine sniffed, then brushed her fingers in Lord Downfield's direction as though she were dismissing a household servant. "I see that I was wrong. Good afternoon, Lord Downfield."

"Good afternoon," Sarah murmured, only for the door to open and a maid to come in with the tea tray, though she squeaked an apology upon seeing the Marquess. Sarah smiled reassuringly and then gestured to the table where she wished the tray to be sat, turning then to ask Lady Catherine to pour the tea.

Lord Downfield, however, had not moved. He had not stepped out, had not made his way out of the room and had not even moved an inch! It was as though he were now fixed in place, as if he had become part of the furnishings of the room and, even when Lady Catherine poured the tea, he still did not move.

A knot tied itself in Sarah's stomach and she let out a long, slow breath as she waited for the gentleman to either say or do something. She glanced to him and then to Lady Catherine who, seeing her look, gave her a light shrug as if to say that she did not know what it was the gentleman was doing but that they should not give him any attention either.

"I do not like to think that my reputation would be so altered in your eyes, Lady Catherine. Nor in yours, Lady Sarah."

Sarah started in surprise as Lord Downfield not only spoke aloud but also then strode across the room towards them, his gaze piercing.

"I should like to bring you something, Lady Sarah," he continued, as she gazed up at him, astonished at his sudden change in character. "What is it that you would like? What is it that would make me appear a little more respectable?"

The knot in Sarah's stomach untied itself as she frowned, recognizing that, yet again, the gentleman was saying such a thing not for her sake but simply to fulfill societal expectations. He did not want her to speak poorly about him to others in society and did not want Lady Catherine to do so either and, therefore, was doing what he could to change that. "I shall bring you whatever would please you."

Sarah shook her head. "There is no need."

"There is every need."

Taking a breath, Sarah looked back at the gentleman directly, hating the arrogance she saw in him. "Lord Downfield, I confess that I do not think your desire to do such a thing is done only because of concern for me. I believe that you are seeking out such a thing in order to make sure that both my friend and I do not speak poorly of you in society and, therefore, your reputation is protected. Is that not so?"

Lord Downfield drew himself up. "I hardly think so."

"And yet, it is as I see it. I must confess, Lord Downfield, that Tom Jones shows himself to be more a gentleman than you and he is only under the patronage of a squire!"

At this, the Marquess frowned heavily, his lips pulling thin. Silence ran between them for a moment or two and Sarah's heart began to beat with a sudden, furious rhythm, realizing what it was she had done. She was not meant to speak of her learning in any way or with anyone and yet, whether he realized it or not, that was precisely what she had done.

"Tom Jones?" Lord Downfield rubbed one hand over his chin. "You compare me to the child of a squire?"

"You do not know him?" Lady Catherine interjected, as Sarah fought to find an answer. "If you had, then you might understand why Lady Sarah has spoken as she did."

A dark shadow drew over Lord Downfield's expression. "I hardly think that being unacquainted with a fellow such as he is something you should be surprised about." The corner of his lip curled. "I am surprised, however, that a lady such as yourself, Lady Sarah, is acquainted with such a fellow. I would have thought that a young lady of quality would have been careful in her acquaintances. Unless, of course, there is a purpose for his connection with you?"

A great and terrible anger ran hot through Sarah's frame, her face growing warm as she took in his words. Was he attempting to suggest that there was something distasteful here? Certainly, he was making it plain that he thought her lesser than him.

"I believe that Tom Jones is acquainted with many gentlemen *and* ladies," she answered, doing all that she could to keep her voice steady. "It is I who am surprised that you do know of whom I speak."

The Marquess' lip curled all the more. "Very well," he said, his shoulders lifting just a little, "I should like to know this fellow, given that you have compared me to him, Lady Sarah. I am surprised – nay, a little insulted – to hear that my behaviour does not match with such a lowly fellow as he!"

An idea came to Sarah, one which spun around her heart and mind and filled her with such a deliciousness that she could barely contain herself. It would be a game, she considered, seeing how Lord Downfield waited for her to respond. A game where she would tease and irritate him in order to make him see that he was not all what he thought himself to be. It would be a breaking apart of his arrogance, a shattering of the hubris she had already seen so clearly. Dare she do it? It would be entertaining but she would certainly have to be careful.

"You asked me what it was that I would like you to bring as a gift, Lord Downfield, is that not so?" Seeing him nod, she continued quickly. "You may pretend otherwise but I know without doubt that you spoke so because you wanted to protect your reputation. You wish for Lady Catherine and I to think well of you so that we will not speak poorly of your behaviour or manner towards me to anyone else. Therefore," she continued, keeping her gaze steady though she twisted her fingers together in her lap so that her courage would not fail her. "Therefore, I *will* tell you what I should like as a gift and Lady Catherine and I will *not* speak ill of you, so long as you are able to decipher a few things which I shall give you."

Lord Downfield blinked. "Decipher?"

"Yes." A little more emboldened, Sarah continued on,

not daring to look at Lady Catherine for fear that whatever expression she would see on her friend's face would prevent her from speaking. "You are pretentious, Lord Downfield. We are barely acquainted and I have already seen your arrogance in full display. Therefore, given all that has been done to me at your hand, and as payment for the damage caused to my foot and the subsequent absence from society, I will give you some mysteries which you must decipher. Mayhap, by the end of it all, you will realise that you are not all what you think yourself to be and will, in future, treat those around you a little more kindly."

There came nothing but silence as Sarah let her words come to a close, her chest heaving with a mix of both nervousness and dread. She swallowed tightly as Lord Downfield's face turned a dark shade of red and he glared at her angrily.

"How dare you?" he breathed, taking a step closer to her. "Do you truly think that I will accept such a thing from your hand? I caused you pain, yes, but it was entirely by accident. You do not know me in the least and – "

"The choice is yours as to whether you accept this from Lady Sarah or not." Lady Catherine's voice was calm and yet commanding at the very same time. "I think it entirely fair that she speaks honestly and openly to the *ton* about all that has taken place and the damage to your reputation which will follow is entirely justified, no? Though," she continued, as Sarah swallowed again, feeling an ache in her throat, "you are being offered an alternative to that which requires you only to think, consider and answer Lady Sarah's questions. The first being that you must discover who Tom Jones is, yes?"

Sarah nodded, watching as Lord Downfield's face grew even redder than before, now a deep scarlet spreading across his cheeks.

"I will not tolerate this," he hissed, his hands curling into tight fists. "Say whatever you wish to the *ton*, I do not care."

"I will say nothing but the truth," Sarah assured him, as he turned on his heel to stalk away. "That is all. I am not about to embellish or to lie, be assured of that."

"I care not." Without another glance towards her, Lord Downfield flung open the door and stalked out of the room, leaving both Sarah and Lady Catherine staring after him.

"Goodness, that was bold of you!" Lady Catherine looked to Sarah who, letting out a long, slow breath, shrugged lightly.

"Yes, it was, but I confess that his arrogance and his disdain towards me has irritated me a great deal. Suggesting that there was more to my acquaintance with Tom Jones was deeply insulting, making it sound as though I was somehow improper!"

"And placing himself on a higher plane than you, certainly," Lady Catherine agreed, shaking her head. "I do wonder if he will agree to what you have suggested, however. He appeared very angry but after some time, it may be that he agrees to what you have said. His desire to have an upstanding reputation is so great that it may be that he cannot turn away from it."

Sarah let herself smile, a relief flooding her now that the Marquess had taken his leave. "Mayhap. Though either way, I should *very* much like to see his face when he realizes that Tom Jones is nothing more than a fictional character in Henry Fielding's novel!"

Lady Catherine began to laugh, her eyes sparkling and, as Sarah imagined what it would be like when that realization hit him, she found herself laughing too. Soon, the room was filled with mirth and all trace of discontent and worry had fled from the room.

Chapter Four

"I can hardly believe she demanded such a thing of me."

Muttering into his glass of whiskey, Matthew took a sip and then another, his brow furrowing. He did not want to have his thoughts captured by Lady Sarah but he could not seem to stop himself from thinking of her. The visit he had endured the previous day had been more than a little frustrating, for he had expected simply to call, make certain that all was well and that the lady was improving, before returning home.

That had not happened. Instead, he had found himself not only insulted but also blackmailed, threatened with the ruination of his character if he did not do as Lady Sarah asked. It was ridiculous, it was foolish and to Matthew's mind, it was most displeasing.

But what if they do as they have said? What if the ton hears them speak badly of me?

The one thing that Matthew reveled in, the one thing that he clung to was his reputation. He was not known as a scoundrel, had not even the smallest hint of roguishness about him and yet, he enjoyed both the company and the admiration of the many young ladies around him. If there was any hint of a disliked character about him, then that admiration might fade and then what would he do?

"You are scowling again."

Matthew grimaced as Lord Rutherford appeared beside him, coming around to sit opposite Matthew, gesturing to the footman for another drink for them both.

"I am permitted to scowl, as I am sure you are aware. Besides," he continued, waving his glass around vaguely, "given that ladies are not permitted in Whites, I hardly think that there is any reason for me to be concerned about my facial expression."

"I suppose that is true," Lord Rutherford agreed, grinning broadly which, for whatever reason, irritated Matthew a great deal. "You were not at Lord Bellington's ball last evening, however. That has concerned me for you were speaking warmly about the prospect only very recently."

Matthew shrugged. "I was not in the right frame."

"Why not?" When Matthew sighed, Lord Rutherford's grin only grew wider. "You know that I will only keep asking until you tell me the truth. I am annoyingly insistent in that way."

"Yes, you are."

"Which you well know. So... ?"

With another sigh – which Lord Rutherford ignored completely – Matthew shared briefly what had happened when he had called upon Lady Sarah. "And so," he finished, "I am left with their blackmail hanging upon me! Either I do as she asks and commit myself to her mysterious questions and the like for a time, or she will speak ill of me to all of London and then where shall I be?"

Lord Rutherford took the glass from the footman's tray and then shrugged. "It does not sound to me as though she is to blackmail you."

"But that is what she has said!"

"No, she said that she would speak to those who asked truthfully about not only what happened but of your behaviour thereafter." Lord Rutherford tilted his head, his eyebrow lifting gently. "You did not think that you would be able to pretend that you were truly compassionate, truly regretful and truly sorrowful over what you did, are you? I have seen you pretend to be those things before and I was not convinced then and I am sure that the lady would not have been convinced either."

"I did and said all that I had to!" Matthew exclaimed, garnering the attention of one or two of the other gentlemen in Whites though he did all he could to ignore them. "There can be nothing wrong with that."

"But you were not sincere."

Deflating a little, Matthew looked away. "Of course I was not."

"And you are concerned now that she will tell her friends and acquaintances of all that has taken place and how you have responded to it. The reason you are concerned about this is because of your reputation amongst the *ton* and, in particular, the ladies of the *ton*. Is that not so?"

"And if it is?"

Lord Rutherford let out a small sigh. "Then you must accept Lady Sarah's request and do what you can to answer the questions – or the mysteries – that she puts to you. That way, she will say nothing and you will be just as admired as you have always been."

Certain that he heard a little weariness in his friend's voice, Matthew frowned hard. "You think that I am foolish."

"I think that you have always been foolish when it comes to expecting the admiration of so many," Lord Rutherford answered, bluntly. "You have built yourself upon being admired, wanting to have the young ladies of London seeing you in the very best way possible, all so that you might feed your pride. But that is something that you have done repeatedly these last few years, so you surely cannot be surprised that I have noticed it?"

A little startled, it took Matthew a few minutes to compose himself enough to answer. Yes, he admitted silently, he had always liked to be admired by the ladies of

London – and respected by the gentlemen also – but had that truly become so significant to him that it was the only thing he considered? And was it so apparent that his closest friend could see it clearly?

"I – I do not want my reputation to be damaged," he said, eventually. "That is all. That is all that I am concerned about."

"Then you will do as Lady Sarah has asked, then," Lord Rutherford answered calmly, as though this was just a simple matter of acceptance. "Though I should say, I do not think it fair that you suggest the lady would lie about you. That is not what she has said, given what you told me."

"But how can I trust that?" Matthew answered, seeing a reason now to do what Lady Sarah had said, a reason which *excluded* his supposed pride. "That is my reason for thinking to do as she asks; it is because she could very easily say a great many dark and unfair things about me to all the members of the *ton* and my reputation could be ruined!" He set his glass down beside him, beginning to gesture now that he had caught onto the notion. "Do you not see that? *That* is why I say that I am being blackmailed. I say it because it is true! Lady Sarah has said that she will say nothing more to the *ton* aside from what has taken place but I do not know the lady and I certainly cannot trust her! She could be nothing more than an idle gossip, looking to put herself as the center, garnering as much attention and sympathy as she can – mayhap to catch the attention of the gentlemen of London so she might then make an excellent match! And it shall be at my expense, at *my* falling that she will do so. Come now, you cannot expect me simply to trust her! I do not know the lady and neither do you."

Lord Rutherford frowned and then ran one hand over his chin, clearly considering. "That is true, I suppose. But all the same, what does it matter if a lady speaks ill of you? It is not as though that has not happened to almost every gentleman in London! Recall that even I had a whisper about me last Season, when Lady Crawford was insulted that I did not dance twice with her daughter? She made up some nonsense and the *ton* where speaking of that for a time though it did soon fade. That is what will happen here, should you decide just to continue on as you are."

"Ah, but I cannot take that risk," Matthew countered. "I cannot be sure that a whisper – whatever it might be – will fade. I cannot pretend that it will go by just as easily as it did for you. Therefore, I should do as the lady has demanded, though I will make certain that these little mysteries of hers are few in number. They cannot simply go on and on until she is satisfied with her scheme!"

Lord Rutherford's frown lingered. "You do speak rather poorly of the lady when she may be quite genteel," he said, mildly. "Might I ask why she has decided to offer you these... mysteries, as you have called them? What was it that made her do such a thing?"

Matthew, who had not explained about Tom Jones, scowled. "She told me that my lack of consideration or some such thing was a good deal lesser than a gentleman who was not even a gentleman! She stated that a fellow named Tom Jones was a better gentleman than I and I, of course, told her that she was utterly mistaken. How could a man without a title be better than I? I, who have been to Eton? It is the most ridiculous thing." Seeing Lord Rutherford's eyes sharpen for a moment, Matthew shifted in his chair, a little uncomfortable. "I may have suggested one or two somewhat ungainly things and that appeared to upset her a great deal."

"Indeed. Though you do not know who Tom Jones is?"

Astonishment wrapped around Matthew's frame. "You

are acquainted with him?"

A light smile tugged at Lord Rutherford's lips. "I am."

"Who is he?" Matthew demanded, sitting forward in his chair. "Surely you will be able to tell me that he is not more of a gentleman than I? Lady Sarah informed that he was taken into the house of a Squire, which does not improve him to me in the least! It means that he has no father or mother to speak of and might very well be illegitimate!"

Lord Rutherford chuckled. "That is something of a mystery, yes. Though I must tell you, I believe that it *is* as the lady says. He is a good deal better mannered than you have been towards Lady Sarah, yes."

Matthew's mouth fell open. "How can you say such a thing?" he breathed, attempting to hide the pain which had lanced his heart. "You are my closest friend and yet now, here you are to tell me that I am no better than a pauper?"

His friend shrugged. "You know very well that I speak as I find so this should come as no surprise to you, my friend."

"But it is... " Matthew squeezed his eyes closed. "Who is he? How is it that you are acquainted with him and I am not?"

"Oh, I am not about to tell you that!" Lord Rutherford exclaimed, chuckling. "My dear friend, this is something that you shall have to find out for yourself."

A bolt of anger lanced through Matthew's heart. "You would do such a thing as that? You, who is my closest friend and – "

"That is the second time that you have called me such a thing," Lord Rutherford interrupted, his tone a little firmer now, "and that should be something of note to you rather than something you throw at me. I *am* your friend. I am your very dear friend, in fact, and I personally think that in pursuing this, you might find yourself somewhat improved."

Insulted, Matthew got to his feet in anger, his hands balling tight. "Improved?"

"Yes," Lord Rutherford said, though he spoke with quietness and did not so much as shift in his chair. "You do not like hearing that from me, but I shall speak my mind nonetheless."

Matthew shook his head, his anger burning so hot, he could not speak. Making a strangled noise, he reached for his glass, tipped the rest of his brandy down his throat and without another word, strode out of Whites and out into the cool night air.

"Improved?" he hissed, walking towards his waiting carriage, his face prickling now with the mixture of heat and fury. "How dare he say such a thing? I need no such improvements! There should be sympathy and understanding rather than agreement." He did not know whether he was angry from what Lord Rutherford had said to him about the need for improvement or whether it was the fact that his friend would not tell him who Tom Jones was, nor how he was acquainted with him. That would have solved a great many of Matthew's difficulties, for then he could have gone to this fellow, acquainted himself with him and discovered what it was about him that made him so much better in his behavior than Matthew himself! Thereafter, he might have been able to go to Lady Sarah, declare that he knew full well who it was she had been speaking of and then, in triumph, declare that he was not about to engage in any other foolishness.

It seemed now, however, that his friend was not about to be of aid to him and, in frustration and anger, Matthew climbed into the carriage and directed it home. He had no time for Lord Rutherford's nonsense at this juncture and certainly had no interest in giving in to all that Lady Sarah demanded.

But neither do I want my reputation to be tainted, he reminded himself as the carriage continued through the dark London streets. *Whatever is it that I am to do?*

***

"Good evening, Lady Sarah."

The white hot streak of anger which raced through Matthew as he bowed in front of the young lady was not unexpected but, all the same, it forced him to clench his hands into fists as he lifted from his bow – though only for a moment so that she would not see.

"Good evening, Lord Downfield," she answered, though she did not bob into a curtsy. "I am afraid that I am unable to curtsy this evening. I can stand and walk a little way without assistance and that is all I am good for."

Matthew managed a tight smile. "I see. Well, it is good to see you in company again." He did not mean this last sentence in the least but all the same, felt himself required to say it, as they were altogether in a ballroom and given the company that they were in. Her mother and father were standing near her, with Lady Catherine by her side though he had not greeted her as yet. Begrudgingly – and having very little inclination towards the light smile on her lips – Matthew inclined his head. "Good evening to you also, Lady Catherine."

"Good evening, Lord Downfield," came the reply, though she said nothing more, that hint of a smile remaining. When Matthew looked again to Lady Sarah, that smile had shifted to Lady Sarah's expression and his frustration redoubled itself. The two young ladies were clearly waiting for something, waiting for him to say that yes, he was doing to do as Lady Sarah had demanded or that no, he was not going to do so and that they could say what they wished about his reputation.

Matthew cleared his throat, hating that he had been bested by Lady Sarah. He was not used to ever having to do as anyone else demanded, had always managed to do just as he pleased without concern or query and yet, here now was this young lady who was nothing but determined to have him do as *she* desired.

What choice to I have?

Despite his anger the previous evening, despite his upset with Lord Rutherford and his singular determination not to give in, after many hours of consideration, Matthew had seen he had no other choice. With a heavy heart and a jaw set in anger, he spread out his hands. "It seems as though I will have to do as you wish, Lady Sarah. Whatever these little mysteries are of yours, I will discover the truth of them. Though you will not be permitted to play games with me endlessly!"

Lady Sarah's eyes gleamed. "Very well, Lord Downfield. How many mysteries should you say are fitting?"

He lifted his chin. "Two."

At this, Lady Catherine let out a snort of obvious disdain. "I should say five. That might bring his pride down a little."

Matthew curled his toes in his boots such was his anger at being spoken about in such a way but he remained silent, nonetheless. This supposed aim of reducing his so-called pride was nothing but foolishness, for to his mind, while there was certainly a little pride in himself, it was nothing in comparison to other gentlemen. It was a trait that every person had, he was sure, and he was no different from any other!

"I think we shall say four," Lady Sarah murmured, tilting her head as her chestnut curls drifted from one shoulder to the next, catching Matthew's attention for a moment. It was only a brief moment but all the same, the anger which had burned through him faded in an instant. He dropped his gaze, trying to bring it back to himself, trying to fill himself with the same fury and upset as he had felt before but nothing came.

"The first is, of course, discovering who Tom Jones is and acquainting yourself with him," Lady Sarah continued, smiling at him and, as Matthew looked back into her eyes, he felt his anger begin to dissipate all the more. "I look forward to hearing what you have learned of him."

Matthew grimaced, looking away. He did not like that she appeared to be so well connected when he was not – and that Lord Rutherford knew of this person also. "You wish me to acquaint myself with this... this *lowly* fellow and thereafter come to inform me that I have done so?"

"Oh no, I wish to know more than that!" Lady Sarah exclaimed. "I wish you to be able to inform me as to why this *lowly fellow*, as you have called him, is a much greater gentleman in terms of his conduct and behaviour than you have been towards me."

His gaze shot back to hers, seeing the smile still gracing her lips. "You speak very boldly for a young lady, demanding such things of me!"

A slight lift of her eyebrows told him that she was less than pleased with his response. "I am afraid, Lord Downfield, that this is what you have agreed to. If you wish to end this before it has even begun, then please, inform me of that now so that I can do as *I* have said I shall do."

"So you can lie about me to all of your friends? So you can spread lies to your companions?" Matthew scoffed, shaking his head. "I hardly think so."

What looked like a flicker of hurt entered Lady Sarah's hazel eyes, her smile fading. "I am not the sort of young lady to lie, Lord Downfield. I have already stated that I would speak only of what has taken place between us, that is all. I would not embellish it, I can assure you."

Matthew hesitated, wanting to tell her that he did not believe her, that he did not believe a single word which she spoke, only for the look in her eyes to convince him otherwise. He stopped himself from speaking so, dropping his gaze and clearing his throat a little gruffly. "Very well, Lady Sarah. I cannot say that I trust you implicitly but I will give you the benefit of the doubt in this situation, at least. All the same, I am not about to turn from what I have agreed to. Instead, I will find this Tom Jones, I will speak with him and acquaint myself with him and, thereafter, will come to speak with you again. Though it may not be the answer that you are hoping for, Lady Sarah. It may be that I find there is nothing significant about his character."

The smile which had been on her lips before returned in an instant, a twinkle in her eye. "I doubt that very much, Lord Downfield, but I suppose I shall accept your answer regardless of my own opinion."

"Good." Feeling a little more in control of the situation now, Matthew clasped his hands behind his back. "Then I look forward to speaking with you again soon. My search shall begin at this very moment." He inclined his head and made to turn away, only for her soft voice to reach him.

"If you wish, Lord Downfield, I might give you a single hint as to where you could find Tom Jones, if you wish?"

A little surprised, Matthew turned back to face her.

"Some benevolence from my captor, then?"

She laughed at this rather than taking offence and, despite himself, Matthew's lips edged up into a half smile though he quickly dimmed it thereafter.

"I am hardly your captor, Lord Downfield, though you may think of me in such terms if you wish." Her eyes still sparkling, she tilted her head. "Do you wish for the hint or not?"

Matthew did not immediately answer. The way that she had laughed, the spark in her eyes and the light color in her cheeks had given him pause. Whether he wanted to notice it or not, Lady Sarah was certainly a pretty young lady, especially when she smiled with such ease. It was only when the moments of silence grew a little uncomfortable and Lady Sarah's eyebrows lifted that Matthew realized he had not yet answered her and, quickly, he shrugged his shoulders. "I suppose so, yes."

"You should not be so generous, not so soon after he has agreed to this," Lady Catherine interjected, putting one hand to Lady Sarah's. "Why must you be so kind?"

Lady Sarah hesitated, then she smiled. "Because what is a little kindness?" she asked, softly, looking to Matthew rather than to her friend. "Now, Lord Downfield, what I must tell you is very important. This fellow, this Tom Jones, can only be found in one place."

Matthew blinked, confusion settling on him. "Only in one place? Does he never make his way to another town or the like?"

"Oh, he does but he still can only be *found* in one place," she answered, her eyes still sparkling with obvious humor though Matthew did not find it in the least bit amusing. "Does that content you or would you like something a little more specific?"

"A little more specific if you please," Matthew grated, as Lady Catherine sighed heavily, her irritation that Lady Sarah was being so kind obviously growing. "Finding him only in one place makes it all the more difficult for I could be searching all over London and *still* be lost."

"Very well." Lady Sarah laughed and tipped her head again, appearing almost a little coy. "He can be found in amongst the shops and the like, in the very heart of London."

Matthew frowned, his jaw suddenly tight. "I find it highly unlikely that a fellow such as he could be discovered in such a place. That is only filled with gentlemen and ladies! Why would a fellow such as he ever dare to walk amongst the *ton*?"

"All the same," Lady Sarah interrupted, her smile now gone and a firmness to her expression which spoke of irritation, "that is where he can be found. Good evening, Lord Downfield. I do hope that you will be able to discover him soon. You might learn a good deal from him."

Scoffing inwardly at this, Matthew kept his expression calm as he bowed. "Good evening, Lady Sarah, Lady Catherine." He made to turn, only for something about the lady's softening expression to catch his attention. For whatever reason, his gaze lingered on her for a brief moment, watching as her lips curved on one side, a slight lift to her eyebrow as she gazed back at him.

And then Matthew turned away completely, his brow furrowing as a flicker of interest in the lady settled in his heart. Frustrated with himself, he made his way directly to the opposite side of the ballroom, determined that he would not be in her company again for the remainder of the evening.

Chapter Five

"Sarah?"

Looking up from her embroidery, Sarah's smile of greeting fixed in place as her father barreled into the room, something in his hand.

"Your father and I would like an explanation for *this*," her mother demanded, flinging out one hand as her father held up a book. "We told you, Sarah, we *insisted* that there would be not a single book in this house and yet here you are, finding yourself another book to read and – "

"It was a gift." Sarah spread out her hands, her shoulders lifting gently. "I could not simply refuse it, Mama, could I?" She watched as her mother looked to her father, a silent exchange going on between them. Her heart began to pound, fear beginning to grab a hold of her. She had not meant to leave the book lying around, had meant to hide it away so that it would not be discovered and yet, somehow, she had managed to do precisely the opposite.

"Who gave you this gift?" Lord Harcastle demanded, his voice low and filled with an anger which Sarah could not hide from. "It is not the sort of thing that a gentleman would bring and therefore, it must have been a friend or acquaintance."

"Yes, it was," Sarah answered, refusing to speak Lady Catherine's name for fear that her parents would refuse to permit the lady to call upon her again. "I have been blessed with a good few visitors since my accident and it was one of them who brought me it. I could not say that I was not permitted such a thing, for that would have brought about a good many questions and I was well aware that you wanted to avoid such things for fear that I would reveal myself to be a bluestocking." This all came out in something of a rush as Sarah tried to recall where that book would have been and how it could have been found. Closing her eyes, she briefly recalled reading it the previous evening before she retired – though it had only been for a few minutes, given that she had been so very tired. In that tiredness, she had clearly forgotten to put her book back in a hidden place and mayhap either the maid had discovered it, or her mother had found it herself when she had come in search of her.

"There was nothing wrong in accepting it," her father said, slowly, his eyes still searching hers as though to make certain that he understood everything, "but thereafter, you should have given it to us. You know that there is an understanding between us – we have taken you to London knowing that there is to be no reading on your part, no furthering of your bluestocking tendencies and if you insist on returning to it, then *I* will insist on returning you to our estate! I do not want to have a bluestocking for a daughter and therefore, it is to be hidden from everyone in society... and clearly, it is not being hidden if you are receiving gifts from acquaintances!"

"It was from someone who knows me well, father, that is all," Sarah said quickly. "It is not as though it is some new acquaintance who has learned this about me."

With a sniff, Lord Harcastle looked away. "I do not like to hear of it, all the same. From now on, Sarah, if you are given a gift of a book, then they are to be immediately given to your mother or to myself so we can place them in the library. Do I make myself clear?"

Wanting to say that she thought her parents were being both a little ridiculous and that there was nothing that would stop her from finding a book to read even if they took every single book from the house and burned it, Sarah simply nodded, not trusting her voice.

"Good." Lord Harcastle seemed to deflate a little, handing the book to his wife. "It is just as well you went to find our daughter this morning, my dear. We might not have discovered this otherwise."

A scratch at the door caught everyone's attention and, after a moment, Lord Harcastle called for the footman to enter.

"Lady Catherine has called," the footman informed them all. "She is waiting in the carriage."

"We are to go to look for some new ribbons for our bonnets," Sarah explained quickly, getting to her feet. "I will be careful on my foot, of course. That is why the carriage has come to take us." She glanced from her mother to her father and, after a moment, Lord Harcastle sighed and then nodded.

"Very well. Though you are *not* to set foot in a bookshop, Sarah."

"I understand," Sarah said, refusing to give him her promise that she would do as he said but all the same, saying something that would content him. "Might I be excused?"

"Are you going with her, my dear?" Lord Harcastle asked his wife but Sarah quit the room just as quickly as she could, refusing to give her mother any time or any reason to join with them. Stopping only for her bonnet and gloves, she hurried into the carriage and sat back opposite Lady Catherine.

"Do hurry," she said, urgently. "I fear that my mother may decide to attend with us after what has been said to me this afternoon!"

Without hesitating, Lady Catherine reached up to rap on the roof and the carriage immediately pulled away. Sarah glanced out of her window, just in time to see her mother coming to stand on the front step of the house, her elbows akimbo and frustration lining her expression.

Letting out a long sigh of relief, Sarah closed her eyes and rested her head back against the squabs.

"Has something happened?" Lady Catherine asked, as Sarah let relief soften every part of her frame. "You appear a little distressed."

"My mother and father found the book you gave me," Sarah explained, opening her eyes. "They told me that I must give them any book that I am given as a gift now. Thereafter, my father reminded me that if I am caught with a book in my possession again, if I am continuing on with my bluestocking ways, then he will have no other choice but to return me to his estate."

"Goodness." Lady Catherine's eyes widened. "Are you quite all right?"

"Of course I am." Sarah sighed and shook her head. "It is disappointing to hear them speak in such a way, I confess, but what can be done? I would much rather that they supported me in my determination to expand my mind as much as I can but if they refuse to do so, then I must do so secretly."

Lady Catherine's eyes twinkled, her lips quirking. "Then I presume you are not in the least bit turned away from the idea of going to the bookshop today?"

"Not in the least!" Sarah answered, spiritedly. "My father stated that I was not to set foot in a bookshop and while I told him that I understood, I did not say that I agreed. Therefore, I have every determination still to go there with you, though I may have to rethink how I am to get those books home! I did not hide my book last evening and that is why it was discovered."

"I am certain that you will think of a way," Lady Catherine answered, glancing out of the window. "Though we can rest as much as you require during our time here at the shops. I do not want your ankle to grow all the more painful."

Sarah smiled. "It is getting better and better every day, I assure you though I thank you for your concern."

Lady Catherine chuckled as she glanced out of the window again. "I wonder if Lord Downfield will spy us here? It may be that he has come to find out this Tom Jones and will spend many hours looking for him." She laughed again as Sarah grinned. "I did think that your little helpful comments to him were very well done though I personally would not have been as generous!"

"I do not know if he was more angry or frustrated once we finished speaking," Sarah answered, as the carriage came to a slow stop. "I think he thought that I would be *very* generous indeed with my clues and yet, when I was not, he appeared all the more upset."

Lady Catherine shrugged. "It will do him good to be spoken to in such a way, even though he does not appreciate it. To be told that you are prideful and that this will do you good must be very difficult to hear, though I know that *I* do not shy away from saying it and that you do not either!"

Sarah laughed again as the carriage door opened. "I do not either, of course. I do wonder how long it will be until he discovers the truth… and how upset he will be thereafter!"

"Indeed. Mayhap we shall go to the milliner's first?"

Sarah nodded. "If we are to go to the bookshop, it must be when it is quiet and when there are not many others present. I do not want any young lady to tell my mother that they saw me there, for fear of what that might do!"

"I quite understand."

So saying, Lady Catherine stepped out of the carriage and Sarah was handed down next. Her ankle twinged as she set her foot on the ground and she winced, catching the concerned look from her friend.

"It will pass in a moment," she said, trying to reassure Lady Catherine. "So long as we walk slowly and not for too long, all shall be well."

"Very well. You may link arms with me too, if that is any help."

Sarah made to do so, only for someone to catch her eye. Her breath hitched, catching in her chest as she looked straight into the face of Lord Downfield. He was some distance away, his brow furrowed and his eyes a little narrowed as though he was displeased about seeing her, but Sarah forced herself not to look away. Instead, she inclined her head just a little but kept her gaze steady, seeing the gentleman do the same.

Then, he began to approach.

"Oh, goodness," she breathed as Lady Catherine caught the movement, looking out ahead of them. "He is so close to the bookshop and so determined, I am sure, to get the answer. Do you think he has gone inside as yet? Do you think he has realised that it is in literature that this gentleman can be found?"

There was no time for her question to be answered for Lord Downfield was within hearing distance and, seeing him still gaze at her, Sarah forced a smile.

"Might I hope that your presence here this afternoon is to introduce me to this acquaintance of yours?" he asked, seeming to forget that there was even a greeting to be offered. "Perhaps you have decided that all of this is nothing more than a foolishness and you are now to bring it to an end?"

"Good afternoon, Lord Downfield," Sarah said, pointedly. "And are you enjoying this fine afternoon sunshine we are enjoying?"

Lord Downfield blinked and then, much to Sarah's surprise, a deep flush began to creep up his neck and into his face. Evidently, he had not realized that he had been a little rude in his approach and now, perhaps realizing so, was a little embarrassed by it. That was interesting, certainly for she had not expected him to be so.

"Good afternoon, Lady Sarah, Lady Catherine." Lord Downfield inclined his head and looked away, even though he had lifted his head from his bow. "I am not, however, enjoying this fine afternoon, given that I have been forced in a hunt where I have very little idea as to where to look."

"That seems a little ungrateful, given that you are now no longer searching through all of London but are, instead, given only a very small place whereby you must search," Sarah answered, firmly. "I do not feel any sympathy for you in this, Lord Downfield."

The edge of his lip curled. "I believe that sympathy is a trait that should be found in every young lady."

A slight flicker of annoyance etched itself into Sarah's expression. "And might I ask if you believe that every gentleman should have the same trait, Lord Downfield?"

His chin lifted. "Of course."

"Then," Sarah answered, warming to the conversation, "you must feel rather ashamed that you showed me so little sympathy when you stood so heavily upon my foot and caused me to wrench my ankle?" She did not look away from him but kept her gaze fixed and steady, her eyes determined and, as the silence grew between them, Sarah's heart lifted in an ever-increasing sense of triumph. Lord Downfield, it appeared, was unable to answer her question and therefore, had chosen to linger in silence. He turned his head, rubbed one hand over his chin and then shook his head before opening his mouth... and then closing it again.

"I think you are without an answer for my friend, Lord Downfield," Lady Catherine interjected, as the gentleman's flushed face began to heat to an even greater color than before. "That is quite all right, you know. You can simply say nothing if you please."

"I am not without words," came the answer as Lord Downfield shot an angry look towards Lady Catherine. "I – I admit that I may have spoken a little hastily there."

"You spoke in the hope of making me feel a little embarrassed about something lacking within myself while refusing to recognise that you had no sympathy whatsoever when it came to the injury you caused," Sarah stated, without hesitation. "Now, as regards your issue with Tom Jones, I will give you no more than I have already given. I do not think it would be fair to do so otherwise."

Lord Downfield said nothing, giving her only a long look, a small sigh and then, with a shrug, made his way from them. Sarah let her gaze linger on him for a few moments longer, taking in his broad frame, his tall stature. He was someone who could easily intimidate others simply by leaning over them or by standing too close but she herself was not about to permit him to do such a thing. She had enough courage within her to stand up to her parents – whether they were aware of it or not – and Lord Downfield was no different, at least not to her mind!

"The milliner's, then?"

Sarah laughed and nodded, linking arms with Lady Catherine and, putting Lord Downfield out of her mind, walked with her friend towards the milliner's.

***

"Do you think that we can step inside now?"

Sarah glanced from right to left. It would soon be time for her to return home so they could prepare for the evening and as yet, they had not stepped into the bookshop. "I – I suppose that we could, yes."

"Do you still want to go?"

Sarah nodded. "I certainly do. There are so many books that I should like to read and new publications that I must simply know about! It does not look as though many of the *ton* are present, so I think that – "

"He is in a *book*?!"

Before Sarah could even make her way into the shop, before she could even step towards the door, it was flung open and a gentleman tore out of it, one finger pointed in her direction.

"I spoke to the shopkeeper and he *laughed* at me!" he exclaimed, as Sarah caught her breath, Lord Downfield's upset a little overwhelming. "He tried to hide it but I could see it in his expression. How dare you trick me in such a way? How dare you pretend that this was someone I ought to be acquainted with?"

Despite the clamoring of her heart, Sarah did not back away, nor did she even step back. Instead, she moved forward, lifting her hand to knock away his finger. "I hardly think that you need to be upset over the fact that you are not well read, Lord Downfield," she said, clearly, her hand clasping his so that he could not point it in her direction again. "That is hardly my fault. I did not ever tell you that Tom Jones was a real and genuine person, did I?"

Lord Downfield blinked, his face red. "I... "

"Did I?" she repeated, a little more firmly now. "Or did I simply make it clear that he was someone you ought to acquaint yourself with? I am surprised to know that a gentleman who has been to Eton had not read Henry Fielding's book!"

Again, Lord Downfield blinked, only for him to step back and then shake his head. "I – I suppose you did not." His voice was quieter now, his eyes no longer holding hers.

"I can see that you are incensed by this supposed duplicity of mine, but I am certain I told you these questions of mine, these little tricks would be *mysteries,* did I not? And if I called them that, then surely you would understand that they were not about to be simple and straightforward?" She squeezed his hand and then released it. "Or was that unclear to you?"

The gentleman did not answer. Instead, he shook his head again, passed one hand over his eyes and then shoved his fingers through his hair, his hat held in the other hand. The sunshine brushed across his fair hair, making it appear almost golden and when he looked back at her, Sarah snatched in a breath.

Despite this moment, despite the tension and the clear upset, there was something about the way that Lord Downfield was looking at her that seemed to pull all of the air from around her so that she could not take in even the smallest amount. She had already admitted to herself that he was handsome but now that they were standing so close, now that they were so near to each other, it was as though she were seeing him in an entirely new light.

It swept over her and Sarah swallowed hard, stepping back so that she could be beside Lady Catherine again. Suddenly, the notion of stepping into the bookshop when Lord Downfield was present was now no longer as welcoming a thought.

"I think we should take our leave, Lady Catherine," she said, looking to her friend who nodded in clear agreement, her gaze a little icy as it swept over Lord Downfield. "Good afternoon, Lord Downfield."

"Wait!" His hand reached out and caught her wrist, sending a rippling shock up over her skin. "I have given you the answer, have I not? I have told you that it is Tom Jones, the literary character in Henry Fielding's novel."

She shook her head, tension raking up her spine. "You have not told me about his character and his behaviour and how it differs from your own," she said, as steadily as she could. "You do recall that this is what was required, I hope?"

Lord Downfield scowled. "But that means that I shall have to read the book."

"And by reading it, further educate yourself," Sarah answered, pulling her wrist from his grip. "That cannot be too bad a thing, can it?" Without giving him a chance to answer, she slipped her arm through Lady Catherine's and, limping slightly, let her friend lead her back towards the carriage.

Chapter Six

Matthew cleared his throat, catching the attention of the bookshop owner who, turning, bowed quickly and then came back towards his desk.

"Yes, my lord?" he asked, smiling. "Might I be able to help you?"

"I – yes." Matthew frowned, uncertain as to how he was to go about asking as to whether or not this fellow was acquainted with Tom Jones. After all, they were in the same class in society and surely that would make them a little more inclined towards being acquainted. If this was where Lady Sarah had said that the fellow could be found, then it might well be that someone here – such as the bookshop owner – would know him.

"My lord?"

Matthew nodded to himself, then looked back to the man. "I wonder if you are acquainted with a man by the name of Tom Jones?"

The bookshop owner blinked, his smile drifting away. "Tom Jones?"

"Yes." Matthew spread out his hands. "I am searching for him. I believe that he was taken in by a local squire as a child. That is all I know of him."

For some reason, a glimmer entered the man's eyes. "Yes, I believe that I do know Tom Jones. He was half in love with a young lady who, unfortunately, was a little out of reach given her situation and his though he did do very well being raised at the Allworthy estate."

Relief washed over Matthew. "Then you *do* know him! Please, where can I find him? I must speak with him over a particular matter."

What sounded like a chuckle escaped from the man's mouth, making Matthew frown hard as his stomach clenched, filled with a sudden misgiving.

"I do believe that, at the end of the story, Tom Jones is discovered to be the nephew of Squire Allworthy and, given that he now has inheritance and standing, he married the lady he loves. They had a son and a daughter too, though that is where the tale comes to an end."

Matthew stared blankly at the fellow, a slight buzzing coming into his ears. He could barely take in what had been said to him, struggling to make sense of all that had been revealed. The man chuckled again, though he rubbed one hand over his mouth at the very same time as if to hide the sound and, all at once, mortification rattled through Matthew's frame, making him drop his head and squeeze his eyes closed.

"Am I to understand" he breathed, "that this Tom Jones is a character in a book?"

The bookshop owner nodded, his eyes dancing though no smile lingered on his face. "Yes, my lord, that is just so. I can fetch you the first book, if you like?"

Matthew blinked furiously. "The first?"

Again, the man nodded, tipping his head as he studied him. "Yes, my lord. There are eighteen sections in total though I should say that it has become a very popular work of late and I expect that it will continue to do well."

Another wave of mortification washed over Matthew and he swallowed hard, turning his head to look out of the window rather than at the man. "If you would be so kind as to fetch me the first part of this novel," he muttered, his hand curling into a fist as he battled his embarrassment. Clearly, this man not only thought it funny that Matthew had come in to ask about a literary character, he now also thought it surprising that Matthew had not even read a part of this supposedly famous novel! A list of excuses sprang into Matthew's mind – he did not read often, it was not part of the expected reading during his time at Eton, he was much too busy with matters of business to spend time reading novels – but he said none of them. There was nothing that would save him from the mortification of this, he could tell.

"At once, my lord."

The man stepped away and Matthew, his gaze now fixed on the window and breathing hard, suddenly caught sight of a familiar face.

Lady Sarah.

She was standing next to Lady Catherine and they were speaking together, though no smile lingered on either face. Fury bit down hard on Matthew's heart and before he could even think, he found himself outside, rushing towards Lady Sarah.

"He is in a *book*?!" The anger which poured into each of Matthew's veins was so strong, he felt his whole frame practically boiling with it as he now stood face to face with the person who had set up this foolish situation in the first place. "I spoke to the shopkeeper and he *laughed* at me! He tried to hide it but I could see it in his expression. How dare you trick me in such a way? How dare you pretend that this was someone I ought to be acquainted with?" Shaking one finger at her, Matthew waited for her response, expecting her to be embarrassed, to be so mortified that she would lower her gaze, drop her head and apologise.

Instead, Lady Sarah reached out, knocked his finger away and grasped his hand as though to stop him raising it at her again, taking a step closer to him as she did so. Her response was clear and unexpected, her gaze fixing to his.

"I hardly think that you need to be upset over the fact

that you are not well read, Lord Downfield. That is hardly my fault. I did not ever tell you that Tom Jones was a real and genuine person, did I?"

"I... " Her hand on his sent a streak of lighting right through him, stealing away his anger in a moment. It was as though her touch had doused his anger completely, leaving him off-balance and ill at ease. He could not give her an answer, her determination to defend herself chasing away all of his defensiveness.

"Did I?" she asked again, her hand pressing his and sending another spiral through him. "Or did I simply make it clear that he was someone you ought to acquaint yourself with? I am surprised to know that a gentleman who has been to Eton had not read Henry Fielding's book!"

Hesitating, Matthew paused and, recognizing that what she had said was quite correct, he closed his eyes and took a step back, shaking his head. There was nothing for him to do but to admit to it, he realized, his own shame beginning to creep upon him as he saw how foolishly he had reacted. No doubt he had quite shocked the lady and, given that his reputation was already a little affected by his previous behavior towards her, this had certainly only made it worse. "I – I suppose you did not." Opening his eyes, he kept them away from the lady, mortification sweeping over him again – though this time, it came from his own shame, his own recognition of his hasty response and his ill-considered actions.

There came slight pause. Lady Sarah, her voice softer now, let out a small breath.

"I can see that you are incensed by this supposed duplicity of mine, but I am certain I told you these questions of mine, these little tricks would be *mysteries,* did I not? And if I called them that, then surely you would understand that they were not about to be simple and straightforward?" She squeezed his hand and then released it. "Or was that unclear to you?"

When she removed her hand from his, a sense of loss tugged at him but Matthew batted it away just as quickly as he could. Every single word she spoke to him was true, Matthew admitted – though he did not say a single thing out loud. Lady Sarah *had* told him that these were mysteries but he had not given that much thought. Evidently, he should have done. Rubbing one hand over his eyes, he pushed his hand through his hair. What was there for him to say to this? Should he open his mouth and admit that he had been wrong? The thought send a rebellion through him and he scowled, refusing to even consider the idea for even a moment longer.

"I think we should take our leave, Lady Catherine." Lady Sarah let out a small sigh and looked back at him. "Good afternoon, Lord Downfield."

A sudden desperation washed over him and reaching out, he caught her wrist. "Wait! I have given you the answer, have I not? I have told you that it is Tom Jones, the literary character in Henry Fielding's novel." He did not release her, something in his heart delighting in the gentle touch they shared and noting that she also had not pulled her hand away. Much to his disappointment, however, Lady Sarah shook her head.

"You have not told me about his character and his behaviour and how it differs from your own. You do recall that this is what was required, I hope?"

A scowl tugged at his features. "But that means that I shall have to read the book." That was the last thing he wished to do. He did not want to waste his precious hours here in London by reading! What he wanted to do very much was spend as much time as he could in the company of those who admired him, who would compliment him and make him feel as though he were the very best gentleman in all of London. Lady Sarah and her foolish games were stealing that from him. *But it is not as though I can turn back now. If I give up, then she will have even more to tell the* ton, *even without embellishment!*

"And by reading it, you will further educate yourself," came the reply as she freed her wrist from his grip. "That cannot be too bad a thing, can it?"

Matthew could not answer that, not wanting to say that yes, it was a good thing while silently aware that it was yet another truth she was offering him. "But there are eighteen sections," he muttered, pushing one hand through his hair before replacing his hat upon his head. He let himself watch her, seeing the slight limp and how heavily she leaned on Lady Catherine. Guilt poured into him, a guilt that he had never really felt before and, disliking the feeling, Matthew turned away. Yes, he admitted, he *had* caused Lady Sarah pain and yes, he had not apologized as he ought to have done but there was no need to feel any sort of overwhelming guilt. He was already suffering consequences because of it, was he not? To have even more now was a foolishness.

"Forgive me for my brief absence. I had someone to speak with." Matthew came back to the man at the desk, seeing a small book set before him. "This is for me, I presume?"

"It is."

"I shall require the rest also," Matthew said, heavily. "It seems that I am to educate myself on this Tom Jones."

The bookshop owner, much to Matthew's relief, did not say a single thing but instead simply nodded and then went in search of the other parts. With a heavy sigh,

Matthew picked up the first book and thumbed through to the first page.

It is a little surprising that a lady would have read such a long novel, he thought to himself, turning the page over to the next. *Though some young ladies do enjoy reading all manner of foolishness, I suppose.*

Sighing inwardly at how much time he would have to devote himself to in order to read this novel, Matthew paid for it all and, a stack now under his arm, stepped out of the bookshop and made his way back to his carriage.

***

"You are reading?"

Matthew looked up as Lord Rutherford sat down opposite him, his eyes wide. "Good evening, Rutherford. Yes, as you can see."

"Goodness. I do not think I have often seen a gentleman spend an evening in Whites with a book in his hand!"

"And yet, I must." Matthew looked up at his friend. "I have discovered Tom Jones."

"Ah." A look of understanding rippled across Lord Rutherford's expression, his lips curving into a smile. "And do you now understand what Lady Sarah was speaking of when she referred to your behaviour being lesser than his?"

Matthew sniffed. "Not as yet," he stated, refusing to admit to anything. "I have discovered that he can sometimes be a drunken lout and that is not in the least bit gentlemanly."

At this, Lord Rutherford rolled his eyes and laughed. "You are so proud that you will not admit that Tom Jones has some better traits than you in how he relates to others?" he asked, pointedly.

Shifting a little uncomfortably in his chair, Matthew set the book to one side and reached for his glass of whiskey. "I will not say that the man does not have some excellent traits," he said, trying to push away the question. "I do not think that I need to say any more than that to Lady Sarah."

"No?" Lord Rutherford shook his head. "I hardly think that she will permit you to have only that as an answer. It seems to me that she is looking for some acknowledgement from you that you have failed where Tom Jones succeeded."

"And why must I compare myself to a fictional fellow?" Matthew exclaimed, his stomach twisting this way and that. "Why must I confess that where he is kind-hearted, I am cold. Where he is sympathetic, I am disinterested, where he is generous, I am selfish. Why must I say such things to her? It appears to me that she knows such things about me already though I would prefer it if she did not have such an impression."

Silence reined for a minute or two, with Lord Rutherford taking a sip of his glass but letting his gaze rove around the room rather than answering Matthew's question. The words that he had spoken ran through Matthew's mind, making him wince as he realized what it was he had admitted to aloud.

"Why is it that you want the lady to have a better impression of you, I wonder?" Lord Rutherford asked, quietly. "Is it solely because of your reputation? Solely because you wish for her to know you better?"

Scoffing at this, Matthew shook his head. "I have very little thought in hoping that the young lady will know me better."

"Then it is because of your reputation."

The gnawing feeling in his stomach returned as

Matthew nodded, choosing to say nothing but instead, looking away. Why was it that he wanted Lady Sarah to think better of him? Was it solely because of his own self-interest? Because he wanted his reputation to be improved upon by both herself and Lady Catherine? Or was there something more? Letting himself think back to the day when she had reached out and caught his hand, almost a sennight ago, Matthew scowled darkly. Yes, he admitted, there had been a rush of feeling but he had not *liked* that sensation. He had not wanted there to be any sort of delight in his heart as regarded her closeness. He found her irritating, frustrating and entirely ridiculous... did he not?

"I think that is what you should say to Lady Sarah," Lord Rutherford said, with a slight lift to his eyebrow when Matthew looked back at him. "I think that you should inform her that yes, you *have* recognised that you were all that you said to me just now. That will content her, whether you mean it or not."

"I *do* mean it." Closing his eyes so as to hide Lord Rutherford's astonished look from affecting him, Matthew forced himself to speak honestly. "I will not pretend any longer. Yes, I was unsympathetic and uncaring as regarded my response to injuring Lady Sarah. I told her that she was the one to blame rather than being apologetic. I knew that it was my fault and instead, I wanted her to take responsibility."

"For what purpose?"

Sighing, Matthew looked back at his friend. "So that my reputation would not be tarnished," he said, simply. "So that no-one began to speak of me as a foolish, clumsy gentleman but instead put all the blame upon Lady Sarah."

His friend nodded slowly. "I see."

"And I am going to have to say this to her, am I not?"

Matthew continued, his whole being rebelling against that idea. "I do not want to but – "

"But if you are to be free of this mystery, then yes."

Matthew chuckled grimly. "Only to be given the next one, yes?"

Lord Rutherford grinned. "Yes, indeed. Though you may not agree with me and no doubt you will be displeased with this but, as I have said before, I think that this will do you good."

Not quite ready to admit to any such thing, Matthew shook his head. "I do not know. Thus far, all it has brought me is embarrassment and frustration."

"Which may serve you well, in the end," Lord Rutherford said, quietly. "When will you speak to her?"

Matthew closed his eyes and heaved a sigh. "Whenever I see her next, I suppose." As he spoke, something flickered in his heart, something that spoke of a faint hope or an expectation of delight in spending time in the lady's company again... but that could not be so, could it? There was nothing about Lady Sarah that he appreciated, nothing about her company he enjoyed and he certainly had no interest in being any longer in conversation with her, he reminded himself, sternly. To let himself feel anything else would be nothing but foolishness.

Chapter Seven

Sarah smiled as she walked with Lady Catherine around the room. "My ankle is entirely better, I must admit. I have not yet danced on it but I am sure that I could."

Lady Catherine smiled at her. "Will your mother permit you to do so?"

Sarah winced. "That, I do not know for certain. She is keeping a very close watch on me this evening, though I am afraid that is not for my benefit. Rather, I believe that she wishes to make certain that I am not being passed any books or the like by anyone!" This made Lady Catherine laugh and, given that Sarah had been a little mirthful, she herself chuckled.

"I hardly think that anyone would give you a book at a ball," Lady Catherine snorted, "though I do find the idea very good indeed. Mayhap I shall find a way to do such a thing and see if she notices!"

Knowing that her friend was joking, Sarah shrugged and then laughed again. "She would snatch it out of your hand before you even had a chance to give it to me, I fear," she answered, sighing just a little. "Though we did not manage to make it into the bookshop as yet, thanks to Lord Downfield."

"Speaking of that gentleman, has he called upon you as yet?"

Sarah shook her head, surprised to find a slight twist of disappointment wrapping about her heart. "No, not as yet."

"Then he must be doing it."

She blinked, a little confused. "Doing what?"

"Reading it," Lady Catherine answered. "He must be reading all eighteen parts to the novel! I confess, I did not expect him to do such a thing. I thought he might simply laugh at the notion and thereafter, refuse to take part in any such thing. I thought that we would be left a little disappointed, having no other fun to enjoy." She elbowed Sarah gently. "It is a little fun, is it not?"

Sarah laughed again, though her face flushed just a little. "Yes, I suppose that it is, though it is a shame that it is at his expense."

"Shame?" Lady Catherine repeated, stopping in her walk and looking at Sarah a little more sharply. "My dear friend, you are doing nothing wrong in this! Lord Downfield is the one who ought to be ashamed of his behaviour and in doing as we are, we are teaching him that he cannot simply expect to treat young ladies – and even other gentlemen – as he does. Whether that will actually be the outcome, I do not know, but all the same, it is something that you must not feel guilty about."

Sarah nodded slowly, seeing her friend frown just a little. "I confess, in seeing him so angry, I did feel a little embarrassed in that regard. I wondered if I should have been a little more benevolent or –"

"You are much too kind, Lady Sarah."

She let out an exclamation and turned sharply, seeing Lord Downfield bowing, a slight smile on his lips. "Lord... Lord Downfield."

"You should not be eavesdropping," Lady Catherine snapped, her eyes narrowing. "It is unseemly."

"You are quite correct, though I was not doing so deliberately. I simply came near and heard you speaking but I should also like to assure you, Lady Sarah, that you need not be concerned. You were already very gracious and I found the answer that you had sent me in search of."

"You have?" Her heart still beating a little more quickly

given the surprise of his arrival, Sarah took him in, seeing the steadiness in his eyes and finding herself a little surprised at how calm he appeared to be. There was not a hint of anger in his expression, his lip was not curling and there were no flickering sparks of fire in his eyes.

"I have." Lord Downfield took in a breath, his eyes darting away from hers for just a moment. "I have read all that was asked of me and I find that it is just as you have said, Lady Sarah. This Tom Jones character was a good deal better a fellow than I, despite his lowly circumstances."

"Indeed?" All the more astonished at the gentleman's acceptance of this, Sarah held his gaze, searching his eyes for the truth.

"Indeed." Lord Downfield sniffed but dropped his eyes to the floor. "I have a cold heart whereas his is evidently a good deal warmer. He has a spirit of generosity within him but I am nothing more than selfish, thinking only of my own ends. He shows sympathy and consideration to others whereas I am nothing but disinterested." He looked back at her then. "There, now. Does that satisfy you?"

Sarah did not know what to say. She could not tell whether he meant every word that he had said or if they were spoken only in the hope that she would take what he had said and be satisfied with it.

"Astonishing." Lady Catherine's voice was dry. "It appears as though you know Tom Jones very well now, Lord Downfield."

"Indeed it does," Sarah agreed, her voice a little quieter. "I confess, I am surprised to hear these determined words from you, Lord Downfield."

He put one hand to his heart. "I am sincere. Though I will tell you that you are not the only one surprised."

Her eyebrows lifted. "Oh?"

"Surprised that a young lady such as yourself would have read so many parts to that one novel," came the reply. "But then again, I reminded myself that young ladies are not given the same excellent standing in education that gentlemen are offered. Mayhap that was the sort of thing that your governess encouraged in you?"

Sarah blinked in surprise, uncertain as to whether the gentleman meant to be insulting or if he was simply stating the facts as he saw it. Doubt filled her as she saw his open expression but a glance to her friend – and to her red cheeks – told her that Lady Catherine at least was certainly insulted.

"My governess taught me a good many things, Lord Downfield," she said, a good deal more firmly than before. "The love of reading is something which has come from within myself, however. I am the youngest of five and had many an hour by which to entertain myself."

Lord Downfield nodded and then shrugged. "I know that young ladies do like to entertain themselves with foolish novels sometimes," he said, making Sarah's anger spark. "It was only the size of the novel which surprised me, though I did enjoy the story."

"Mayhap you think I should be reading about the latest developments in crop rotation?" Sarah asked, sharply. "Or about the most recent artworks which have been displayed in Italy? Or are those things only for the gentlemen of the *ton*?"

Lady Catherine cleared her throat and instantly, Sarah realized that she had spoken a little foolishly. There was no concern in her mind that Lord Downfield would take what she had said and realize that she was bluestocking but, all the same, she needed to be more careful.

Lord Downfield frowned, looking at her steadily. "I do not know much about art, I am afraid. Crop rotation, however, is something that I have been reading about but yes, I suppose that is something that I would only expect of a gentleman."

Sarah lowered her head. "Quite."

A silence prevailed for a time, only for Lord Downfield to cough quietly, forcing Sarah to lift her head.

"Well?"

She frowned. "Well?"

"The next task? Your next mystery?"

"Oh." Sarah blinked and looked to Lady Catherine, who only shrugged. Too late, she realized, she had not thought of what was to be next for Lord Downfield. "I am afraid that I am not certain, as yet. Though mayhap, since you say you know very little about art, I should make it on that very subject?"

Lord Downfield, much to her surprise, chuckled. "So long as it does not require me to read eighteen parts of a novel again, I shall be glad to do whatever you wish, Lady Sarah."

Finding herself quite taken aback at this change in his demeanor towards her, Sarah paused for a moment, looking again to Lady Catherine who only offered her a very small smile in response. "I will consider and have something for you come the morrow, Lord Downfield. Does that satisfy you?"

He nodded. "Indeed it does." He glanced to the floor at her feet, then looked back up at her. "Might I ask, Lady Sarah, if your ankle is entirely recovered?"

"It is." It was the first time that he had asked about her ankle since the accident and, given the expression on his face – the concern in his eyes and the frown on his forehead – Sarah believed him to be genuine. "Thank you for your concern, Lord Downfield."

"It is a little late in coming, is it not?"

The answer surprised her all the more and she responded only with a small smile, not quite certain what to make of the gentleman before her. Was this the very same fellow who had roared in anger at her only the previous sennight? The one who had laughed and berated her when *he* had been the one to stand on her foot due to his own lack of consideration?

All the same, he was still a little insulting and demeaning, though he may not have meant to be, she reminded herself, as the music for the next dance began. *This may all be a pretense. I cannot be sure of anything.*

"Might you wish to dance, Lady Sarah? Only if your ankle permits you, of course. It might be a good way for the *ton* to see that there is no malice between us. I know that some are still speaking of what happened that evening."

"You wish to dance with me?"

Lord Downfield nodded. "Of course."

"Only to show society that you are in good standing with Lady Sarah, however," Lady Catherine murmured, making Sarah's heart sink low. "Is that not so?"

Lord Downfield spread out his hands. "It is only one dance, Lady Catherine. Should you like to stand up with me also, I would be glad to sign your dance card."

Lady Catherine laughed and shook her head. "No, I thank you. You have no need to stand up with me, Lord Downfield, for I was not the one you injured. I am not the one that you must now be seen out dancing with, in the hope that the *ton* will think just as well of you as they always did."

Sarah, a little frustrated with herself that she had let her heart leap in such a fashion, offered him a tight smile. "I do not think that such a dance is necessary. The *ton* can think as they please. It does not give me even a moment of concern."

Lord Downfield frowned, his mouth twisting just a little. "I do not mean to suggest that the only reason for my request is because I wish for the *ton* to think better of me, Lady Sarah. Forgive me if that is what you now believe. That is certainly an aspect, I will be honest in that, but I should also like simply to stand up with you. I have not danced in some time and it would give me great pleasure to do so now."

Her foolish heart leapt up again but Sarah quietened it in an instant, refusing to let herself believe that Lord Downfield had a genuine interest in dancing with her. This was all about society and what they thought of him, she was sure. "Very well, Lord Downfield. We shall dance."

A smile spread right across his face that send a glimmering light into his eyes. "Are you quite sure?"

The expression on his face, the happiness in his eyes and the warm smile made Sarah's heart leap up all over again and this time, when she took his hand, Sarah could not quieten it. She glanced to Lady Catherine, offering her a slightly wry smile but her friend only frowned, clearly displeased that Sarah had decided to agree to Lord Downfield's request. Her mother, who had been standing nearby, also caught Sarah's attention but there was clearly no concern there, given the way she smiled. "What dance is it, Lord Downfield?"

He looked at her. "The waltz, I believe."

Sarah's heart immediately slammed hard against her ribs, her eyes going to his again but Lord Downfield was already looking away. She had not thought to ask him about what the dance was beforehand, had agreed to it without even thinking and now she was to be wrapped in his arms in the waltz?

"I do promise to be very careful indeed where I step," he murmured, standing back from her and bowing as the couples all took to the floor. "I do not have heavy feet when it comes to the waltz, Lady Sarah, and I have every intention of proving that to you."

Sarah barely managed to curtsy before Lord Downfield had stepped forward, his hand settling at her waist and his other hand grasping hers lightly. She had not danced the waltz since the previous Season and even then, it had only been once. Fearful that she would not remember the steps and would make a fool of herself, Sarah tried to keep herself steady, her fingers tightening around Lord Downfield's.

"You need not worry so much, Lady Sarah. You are doing very well."

Astonished that he had seen her concern, Sarah looked up into Lord Downfield's face, seeing him smile at her.

"The waltz is the easiest dance, I assure you," he told her, his voice holding a gentleness which she had never heard before. "All you must do is trust me to lead you – and lead you I shall."

Sarah said nothing, looking up into his eyes and letting herself sink slowly into the dance, trusting him to lead her as he had promised. The steps began to come a little more easily, the tension left her frame and Sarah let a sense of relief wash over her.

"There now," Lord Downfield murmured, as he spun her lightly around the floor. "You are much more contented now, yes?"

"Yes, I am," Sarah managed to say, her voice a little breathy and light. "Forgive me, I had not danced the waltz in some time and I was a little concerned that I might be the one to stand on *your* foot this time."

At this, Lord Downfield chuckled and Sarah laughed

along with him, her heart now settled and calm. The waltz continued on in silence but Sarah's smile lingered, telling that she was enjoying this moment, even though it had come unexpectedly. When it came to an end, she was almost a little regretful, stepping back from him and, this time, dropping into a proper curtsy.

"Permit me to lead you back to your mother and your friend," Lord Downfield said, offering his arm.

She took it. "I think that the *ton* will be more than satisfied now, Lord Downfield," she remarked, silently reminding herself that this was the reason he had asked to dance with her, even though that thought brought her a streak of sorrow. "We have danced and they will be assured that there is no animosity between us. Your reputation is spared, certainly."

Lord Downfield turned his head and looked at her, his steps slowing for a moment. He opened his mouth, then closed it again before shaking his head, a heavy frown pulling down his eyebrows. "I did not think of that, not even for a single moment during our waltz," he muttered, as if he was speaking half to himself rather than to her. "I enjoyed it very much."

"As did I," Sarah admitted, though she kept her gaze away from his, heat beginning to suffuse her cheeks as she spoke. It was as though, in saying such a thing to him, she was informing him that there was a happiness within their connection, though she herself had never expected such a thing. Pushing that feeling away, she took her arm from his and gave him a brief nod of farewell. "I thank you, Lord Downfield. Do excuse me."

"But of course," he murmured, having now deposited her beside her mother. "Good evening, Lady Sarah."

"Good evening."

Chapter Eight

"You say you are waiting for her next mystery to be given to you?"

Matthew nodded. "Yes, I am."

"She was surprised at your revelation, then?"

A small smile touched Matthew's mouth. "Yes, indeed."

"Though you did not mean a single word of it, I suppose?" Lord Dover remarked, as Matthew shot him a quick look. The gentleman shrugged and indicated Lord Rutherford. "He and I may have been talking about your situation and the difficulties that are presented with it at the present movement."

Lord Rutherford shrugged. "I informed him that you had a great deal to say to Lady Sarah but that you were not going to mean a single word of it."

"Except, I did."

The moment those words left his mouth, Matthew blinked in surprise, his eyes rounding as astonishment filled him. He had not meant to say anything like that, had not meant to express any sort of truth to his friends and now found himself a little embarrassed by it.

"You… you did?" Lord Stephenson, who had only recently come to join their conversation as they stood in Hyde Park, sounded almost upset. "I did not think that you would be willing to admit to anything like that. From what I understood, you were deeply frustrated with all that Lady Sarah had put to you."

"I was… I am, of course." Matthew cleared his throat as he attempted to sort out his thoughts, one from the other. "It is only to say that what she said of me was, much to my frustration, quite true. This figure, this literary character showed more sympathy, consideration and kindness than I ever had. That is not something that I could continue to pretend was not true." He looked away and lifted his shoulders. "Besides, if I had said such things to her without ever really meaning them, I am quite certain that Lady Sarah would have been aware of it. And then I would have been dragged through further questions and the like and I was certainly not interested in doing such a thing as that! No, I would much rather get on since I have three mysteries still to go until she is done with me." He did not say a word to any of his friends as regarded his present feelings for the lady, finding that they were confusing him and, in a way, upsetting him greatly. He did not want to have anything other than irritation directed towards Lady Sarah and yet, as they had waltzed, he had found his heart beginning to quake with a sense of delight, of a happiness which he had never expected to feel.

"I suppose that makes sense," Lord Dover said, after a short silence following Matthew's words. "She certainly has a great many demands, does she not? I am surprised that you are enduring it so well and without any great complaints!"

At this, Lord Rutherford snorted. "He has been complaining a great deal, Lord Dover. It is only that you have not been around to hear it!"

Matthew opened his mouth to protest, only to close it again as he offered nothing more than a wry smile. Lord Rutherford was quite correct, despite Matthew's desire to pretend he had not said a single word of complaint as regarded the situation.

"Do you know what her next mystery is to be?" Lord Stephenson's interest played out in his voice. "I must say, this first one about Tom Jones does have me somewhat intrigued. What sort of young lady reads all eighteen parts of that novel?"

"A young lady who enjoys reading, I would think," Matthew found himself saying hastily, a defensiveness over the lady beginning to wash over him. "She is the youngest of five children and evidently, had a good many hours by which she might read." His three friends turned to look at him and, seeing the slight surprise in each of their eyes, Matthew flushed hot. "The next mystery, however, is to do with art of some sort. I do not know what precisely but it is something to do with the French, that much I know."

"The French?" Lord Rutherford repeated, as Matthew nodded. "Goodness, Lady Sarah must be very well informed as regards the latest offerings of art in France, for even I do not know a great deal about that."

Matthew considered this as his other friends made much the same remark, silently wondering how it was that Lady Sarah was, in fact, so highly educated. Yes, it was clear that she loved to read but he had only ever considered that she would read novels and other foolishness. Surely she would not be reading articles about art nor, as she herself had said, about crop rotation? That was not something that a young lady ought to be reading, surely?

"There she is."

Matthew jumped as Lord Rutherford touched his arm, pulling him out of his thoughts. "I beg your pardon?"

"There is Lady Sarah," Lord Rutherford explained, gesturing to her. "Do you wish to ask her what her mystery is for you? That way, you can begin to proceed and remove yourself from this situation all the more quickly."

A sudden lurch of Matthew's heart left him a little off balance and it took him a moment to gather himself. It was almost as though he were pleased to see her, almost as though he was already happily anticipating being in her company. Surely one dance with her could not have brought about this sudden change? It seemed that, after he had spoken with her, after he had admitted to her all that he had recognized about himself in comparison to Tom Jones and after they had danced together, his heart towards her had entirely changed.

It was most disconcerting.

"Yes, I suppose I shall. You are quite right." Fearful that his friends might notice something in his expression should he linger even a moment longer, Matthew strode directly towards Lady Sarah who was, as always, in the company of Lady Catherine.

"Good afternoon, Lady Catherine, Lady Sarah." He bowed low, only for the two ladies to exchange a glance, with Lady Sarah offering him a bright smile.

"It seems as though you have remembered that you are to greet us first, rather than simply beginning your conversation," she remarked, a twinkle in her eye. "Mayhap you will now go on to ask if we are enjoying the afternoon or if we find the fashionable hour too busy?"

Matthew found himself smiling, despite the wry tilt of her lips. "On this occasion, I shall have to disappoint," he said, as Lady Sarah laughed. "I have, instead, come to ask if you have your second mystery for me, Lady Sarah? I should like to begin my next assignment, if you can call it that."

Lady Sarah tipped her head, her hazel eyes full of vivacity and life. When she smiled, it was as though the sun shone a little warmer, her curls dancing lightly in the soft breeze. Matthew swallowed hard and looked away, all the more astonished and confused by this strange feeling which was now beginning to take a hold of him all the more strongly. He did not want this game to continue, he reminded himself. He did not *want* to take part in any further games that Lady Sarah had for him.

So why do I find my heart leaping in hope and anticipation?

"Very well." Lady Sarah glanced to Lady Catherine, who gave her what appeared to be a reassuring nod. Did she feel some sort of concern in speaking as she did? Or was this nothing more than friendly solidarity?

"There is a new exhibition in Paris, one which features a particular artist, though, sadly, the artist is no longer with us. This work is to be shown for some time and, I believe, will show some pieces which have never yet been seen by society. It is a rather exciting moment and I confess, my own interest has been piqued in reading of it."

"And you wish for me to know the name of this painter?"

Lady Sarah smiled. "Ah, I did not say this person was a painter now, did I?"

Matthew paused for a moment, considering. "No, you did not. Though I do hope you do not expect me to make my way to France in order to discover the truth?"

At this, Lady Sarah laughed gently and Matthew's face broke into a smile – a smile which sent a flurry of delight all through him. Lady Sarah's eyes were dancing and though he had seen such an expression upon her before, he had never felt himself so happy with it. When she had first laughed in his company, he had taken it to be mockery, a teasing which he had been utterly displeased with.

His brows furrowed and he looked away. *And I was wrong to think that. I jumped to a hasty judgement and considered the lady very poorly indeed.*

"Oh, good gracious, Lord Downfield, do not look so concerned!"

A soft hand touched his and Matthew looked up quickly, seeing the concern now in Lady Sarah's eyes.

"I will not expect you to go to France, of course not! The news of this exhibition has been in many publications and I am certain you will be able to find it without too much difficulty."

Matthew smiled quickly, wanting to remove the worry from her expression. "That is a relief. I shall go on with my considerations at this very moment, Lady Sarah." When she took her hand away from his, Matthew clasped his own behind his back, trying to ignore the way that warmth had run from him, crashing away from him. "Thank you, Lady Sarah. Good afternoon to you both."

With a nod and a smile, Matthew turned away, only to walk almost directly into Lord Rutherford who was, Matthew noticed, not looking at him but instead, directing his attention towards Lady Catherine.

"I do hope you were not about to take your leave? I was only just coming to join you!" Lord Rutherford exclaimed, as Matthew was forced to turn back, a little astonished at the warmth in his friend's voice. "Might you be so good as to introduce me, Downfield?"

Shaking off his surprise, Matthew quickly did so, and almost immediately, Lord Rutherford began to strike up a conversation with Lady Catherine, leaving Matthew himself as well as Lady Sarah, to stand quietly and simply listen. Try as he might, Matthew could not think of what he might say to the lady in order to begin a new conversation and, as the minutes dragged on, the more uncertain and confused he became. He did not know what to do nor what to think. He was now standing beside Lady Sarah, a hint of sweet honey in the air which he was certain came from the lady herself, and his entire being was beginning to burn with a confounded heat which he was sure did not only come from the sun.

He glanced at her, seeing her give him a brief smile before turning her gaze away again.

Why can I think of nothing to say?

"Might I ask you something, Lord Downfield?"

Relief poured into him as he turned to face Lady Sarah entirely, nodding fervently. "I should be delighted if you would." Was it just his own mind or was there a light flicker of color in her cheeks?

"Have you been to France before? My brother went on the Great Adventure and came back with a good many stories which quite ignited my imagination!"

"To France?"

She nodded.

"I have, yes." Warming quickly to the conversation, Matthew began to talk about all he had seen and heard during his time in France and in other countries besides. "I too went on the Great Adventure, as so many gentlemen do when they are a little younger – before they are then in search of a wife – and found it a most enjoyable experience."

Lady Sarah smiled and then let out a soft laugh. "I think that must be quite true what you say about gentlemen going there before they are in search of a wife, Lord Downfield. My brother returned from his Great Adventure and, thereafter, found himself engaged within the month! He is quite contented now."

"I am glad to hear it."

"Though you have not done the same as he," Lady Sarah continued, quietly, her eyes searching his face. "You have not returned home and immediately found yourself a bride."

Matthew did not quite know what to make of this. Was it a simple observation on her part or did she mean something more by it?

"We certainly *shall* dance at the very next ball, Lady Catherine, I can assure you of that!"

Lord Rutherford's exclamation caught Matthew's attention and, much to his relief, the end of the conversation soon followed thereafter. Lord Rutherford bid farewell to Lady Catherine and to Lady Sarah and Matthew added his own farewell to it though his mind remained filled with questions as regarded Lady Sarah's last remark to him. Had she simply been making a note of something, remarking upon it as any young lady might do? Or was there a hint of interest, of hope there?

"I do think her a very fine young lady. Thank you for introducing me."

Coming back to himself rather than remaining lost in thought, Matthew looked to Lord Rutherford who was doing nothing but grinning broadly. "Lady Catherine?"

"Of course Lady Catherine!" Lord Rutherford slapped Matthew on the shoulder, his eyes sparkling. "I must say, she is a very fine young lady indeed! I am looking forward to dancing with her already." His smile dropped just a little though a flicker of interest remained in his eyes. "I noted that your conversation with Lady Sarah was not altogether terrible. Might it be that things are a little improved between you?"

"Mayhap a little," Matthew answered, refusing to divulge even the smallest amount of the new consideration he had for the lady. "Though I must say, I am surprised to see you so taken with Lady Catherine so quickly!"

Lord Rutherford chuckled, his attention quickly diverted from the conversation about Lady Sarah. "I did not realise she was as beautiful as she is! I have heard you speak of her tenacity –"

"Her blunt manner and sharp tone," Matthew interjected, though Lord Rutherford simply waved that away.

"And since I had opportunity now to be introduced, I thought I should take it. I must say, she is a remarkably fine lady indeed!"

"Mayhap your opinion will change when you are on the receiving end of the sharp edge of her tongue," Matthew remarked dryly but Lord Rutherford only laughed. The conversation continued on but Matthew's thoughts lingered on Lady Sarah. Their conversation *had* been very pleasant indeed and though he told himself he ought not to be letting his mind continue to think on her, Matthew could do nothing but that for the rest of the afternoon.

Chapter Nine

"That Lord Downfield has been paying you a good deal of attention of late, Sarah."

Sarah looked back at her mother without altering a single part of her expression, her lips curved in a soft smile. "Yes, Mama. It would seem that he has."

"He is often in conversation with you and has danced with you once already – and it was the waltz, was it not?"

Sarah nodded, ignoring the light butterflies in her stomach. "Yes, Mama, it was. Though he has not repeated that since."

"Oh, but that does not mean anything!" Lady Harcastle exclaimed, as the carriage took them to Lord and Lady Murchison's ball. "He might ask you this evening and you must, of course, say yes." She waved one hand vaguely. "I am aware that he was the gentleman who caused your ankle a great injury at the very beginning of the Season but that may have gone in your favour! It seems now that his apology might have turned into an interest in you!"

Sarah offered nothing more than a smile, looking away rather than permitting her mother to examine her expression for fear of what she might see there. There had been a change in her connection with Lord Downfield, that she was sure, but what it was as yet, Sarah could not quite understand. They had engaged in a few conversations and she had found him more than amiable, with not even the smallest hint of frustration or anger which she had seen in him before. It was as though, in spending the time reading and considering the difference between Tom Jones and himself, Lord Downfield's character itself had begun to alter!

Unless he was always that sort of fellow but his pride

affected his character in the most dreadful way.

"I do hope that he will dance with you again this evening," Lady Harcastle hummed, as Sarah hands curled in her lap, her heart quickening at the thought. "I should like that very much."

I should like that too, Sarah admitted to herself, a faint heat in her cheeks. The carriage continued to roll onwards and finally came to a stop just outside the house and Sarah let out a breath of relief, glad now that the conversation about Lord Downfield would come to an end. It was confusing enough for her to only think about and to speak about it also would only cause it all the more, she was sure!

"I must also ask you, Sarah, whether you have been speaking of your learning to anyone?"

Sarah turned to her mother who had descended from the carriage, following her question. "No, Mama, I have not."

"Are you quite certain?"

A little confused, Sarah nodded. "I am certain I have not said a word to anyone."

Her mother's eyes slanted towards hers for a moment before turning back again to the house in front of them, stepping towards it as Sarah followed her. "The reason I ask is because Lady Carmichael told me she heard you discussing French art with both Lady Catherine and a gentleman or two?"

A slight hint of panic trapped itself in Sarah's heart. "Lady Carmichael overheard this? I am surprised that she would think to eavesdrop."

"She did not eavesdrop, Sarah," her mother answered, a little more sharply. "Sometimes it is impossible *not* to overhear a conversation given how closely we stand with someone else, that is all." She turned to face Sarah now, standing at the foot of the steps which led to the house. "Tell me the truth. Were you discussing art?"

Sarah lifted her chin, refusing to give into the panic which was now threading through her. "Mama, I was discussing my brother's ventures during the Great Adventure. France was certainly discussed and I know that art was mentioned but that may not have been by me. Besides which, even if it was, I would only have been agreeing with whatever else was said, stating that my brother had seen the very same." Seeing her mother frown, Sarah spoke hastily, her fingers knotting together as she clasped her hands in front of her. "I should say, Mama, that this was in discussion with Lord Downfield for he was certainly present at the time. Given his interest, I was not about to stay silent, of course. I had to make certain I spoke of what I knew but I was very cautious."

At this, Lady Harcastle's eyebrows lifted, pulling the frown from her face. "I see. Well, that is quite different, is it not?" She offered Sarah a smile and then hurried up the stairs, leaving Sarah to trail after her, suddenly weak with relief that her mother was no longer to quiz her on what had been said and what she had told the gentleman. All the same, Sarah reminded herself, she had to be a good deal more careful in where she was standing whenever she spoke to Lord Downfield. The last thing she wanted was to be pulled away from society... and from Lord Downfield too.

***

"I have it!"

Sarah jumped in surprise, only to smile brightly as Lord Downfield's grinning face greeted her. "Lord Downfield, good evening."

"I – oh." With a quick bow, he clasped his hands

behind his back. "Good evening, Lady Sarah. I do hope that you are enjoying the ball this evening?"

Sarah laughed, seeing his eyes round a little in surprise. "You are certainly doing your level best to be gentlemanly, are you not? Though I do not think that on this occasion, it is required. You have clearly some excitement about you – it is about the... " She frowned, turning her head to one side and then to the other, seeing just how close they were to others. "Is it about what we discussed?"

Lord Downfield nodded, though his smile was no longer as bright, his eyes holding gentle confusion rather than happiness. "It is. Are you quite well?"

Sarah nodded. "Might we move to the back of the ballroom, Lord Downfield? Lady Catherine will return soon enough and will come in search of me, I am sure, and my mother is only a little away."

The gentleman's eyes rounded and Sarah dropped her head, mortification filling her.

"I mean only so that I can hear you clearly, rather than for any other reason," she added, hastily. "There is so much noise here, so many voices and music that I feel as though I have to strain to hear you."

"Ah." Lord Downfield nodded. "Of course. Please." He held out one hand to his left and Sarah quickly stepped away, silently praying that her mother would not notice her and follow. It was only a few steps and they were then in the shadows of the room, though in clear sight of Lady Harcastle still. Relieved, Sarah turned to face Lord Downfield again, her worries no longer present.

"You were about to tell me that you knew the answer to the question I posed you?"

Instantly, Lord Downfield's face split with a smile. "I did, though I confess, it did not take me as much time as I feared it would! A little reading, a little conversation and I discovered that the fellow – may he rest in peace – was none other than Antoine Watteau!" He reached out and caught her hand. "I must tell you, I found myself quite captivated with some of his works. The landscapes in particular were very beautiful. I do remember seeing some of his work previously during my Great Adventure but I had never taken any great interest in him. I was glad to be afforded the opportunity now."

"I am delighted to hear it! I confess that I have not seen his work in any real detail, only heard of it from my brother and from what I have read. I have heard that there is often a great wistfulness in his works."

Lord Downfield smiled. "There is. I should like it if you could see his works one day, Lady Sarah. I think that your heart would understand them in a way that my own does not."

Sarah was not quite certain what to make of this comment, though she considered it to be a compliment. She smiled back at him and for some moments, nothing was said. Sarah found herself quite comfortable in the silence, looking into the gentleman's eyes and silently wondering what she had ever found about him to be so dreadfully disagreeable.

"Well?" His tone was softer now and Sarah blinked, a little uncertain as to what he meant. When she did not answer, he chuckled, his hand shifting on hers and making her realize that as yet, he had not released her fingers from his. She swallowed quickly, the warmth of his grip thrilling her though she dared not let a single emotion flicker across her face. Was he asking her for something more? Something that might grow from this warmth which she now felt spreading across her chest, the warmth which came from his hand holding hers? Dare she say that she was enjoying his company, that she found herself in a place where she had never once expected?

"The next mystery?" he asked, making Sarah flush with embarrassment as she realized what he meant – and that it was not what she had hoped. "If you have not yet thought of it, then that is quite all right." He tilted his head. "I find that I am no longer in as eager a hurry as I was before."

"That is good, I think," she answered, her voice quavering just a little given the way that one emotion jumped over another. "I confess that I have not thought of any as yet, though… " She paused, wondering if she dared to trust him with this. "I – I should like to ask that anything we discuss on this matter be kept as private as could possibly be? Not because I am ashamed of it but rather because I have had my mother coming to me with remarks that another person has made over a previous conversation – the one about the French artist – and I should not like any gossip to follow."

This was not exactly what concerned her, of course, for she was worried that someone would hear of her discussion with him as regarded the knowledge she had gained from her reading and her mother would, thereafter, pull her from society. Lord Downfield, however, made very little by way of concern and instead, simply nodded.

"But of course, I quite understand. That is wise thinking, Lady Sarah." He looked down at their joined hands and, with a quiet cough, released her. "Gossip is something that I utterly despise."

"It is. I – "

"Ah, there you are!"

A gentleman that Sarah did not recognize hurried over to them both, making Sarah's eyebrows lift as the gentleman completely ignored her and instead, put a hand to Lord

Downfield's arm.

"I have been looking all over for you! The Duchess of Kettering and her daughter, Lady Alice, are busy discussing the gentlemen of London and, given your standing in London, I thought you might wish to go and join them so that they might... well, you understand what I mean!"

Sarah's shoulders dropped, her lip curling. Surely Lord Downfield would not simply abandon her here to go and stand with a young lady of higher standing? She knew that pride had certainly been a great concern to him of late but she had thought, since his change in attitude towards her, that this might now have altered him all the more.

She was to be disappointed.

"Lady Alice?" Lord Downfield suddenly seemed to rise an inch or two taller, his chest puffing out, his eyes searching the crowd as the other gentleman nodded fervently. "You say that they are discussing the gentlemen of London?"

"They are, for everyone has heard them. They seek to know which are the very best fellows in all of London – though I do not know if they do that for their own pleasures or if they do it because they do wish to consider the gentlemen who might make a match with Lady Alice – but all the same, it is being loudly and obviously discussed."

"Then I must go at once! Thank you for informing me, Lord Dover. You clearly know me well enough to understand that this is a situation I simply *must* be a part of!"

Much to Sarah's dismay, the gentlemen both walked off together, with Lord Downfield not so much as turning his head to look at her. He had not bidden her good evening, had not told her that he would return to continue with their conversation... he had said nothing. She was left now with silence, with a heaviness in her heart and the heat of shame rippling down over her in waves. It was not as though she were ashamed by anything that *he* had done but that she had become ashamed of her own foolishness as regarded the gentleman.

I let his improvement affect me, she recognized, lowering her head and then squeezing her eyes closed. *There has been change, yes, but clearly he is not altered enough to truly consider me… or mayhap this has all been nothing more than a pretense ever since it began! Have I been foolish in letting myself become altered in my view and consideration of him?*

A little surprised to see tears forming behind her eyes at this, Sarah took in a deep breath, sniffed and then lifted her chin. The last thing she needed was for her mother to notice that she was upset, for that would lead to a good many questions… and Sarah was quite sure that she did not have the answers for any of them.

Chapter Ten

Having already greeted the Duchess, Matthew bowed low towards her daughter. "Good evening, Lady Alice. How very pleasant to be in your company again."

Lady Alice cast a disparaging eye over him. "It seems that we are already acquainted, Lord Downfield, though I confess that I do not remember you."

Matthew blinked, a little stunned by the young lady's coldness. At the same time, a hint of concern began to wrap around his heart, spreading down cold towards his fingertips. He glanced surreptitiously to his right and then to his left, a little concerned that there would be those nearby who would overhear Lady Alice as she spoke of him in such a way. "I – I am sorry to hear that," he stammered, all the more embarrassed. "I did not think... that is, I did not know that I had not made a particular impression upon you." Forcing a smile, he spread out his hands either side as the Duchess continued to watch the interaction with careful eyes. "Mayhap I can make up for that now?"

Lady Alice arched one eyebrow. "Mayhap, though I am not certain that you will succeed, Lord Downfield."

"No?" The smile he had fixed to his face was all the more difficult to keep in place as the worry in his chest began to grow and spread. "I am sure that you have a good many admirers, Lady Alice, but there must be some who are deemed favorable in your eyes! Let us hope that I can be one of them."

All that he received by way of answer was a sniff. Heat spread out across his chest and up into his neck, glancing all around him again and catching one or two of the other guests looking at him, worried now that what they had heard

Lady Alice say would now spread across London society. That familiar concern, the importance of being well spoken of, of being highly regarded by everyone in the *ton* slammed back into his heart and Matthew took in a deep breath.

"Tell me, Lady Alice, what interests have you? Mayhap we will have a shared enjoyment and can discuss that in conversation which would, I am sure, bring us both a good deal of pleasure."

Lady Alice looked away. "I do not think embroidery is something that a gentleman pursues, Lord Downfield."

"No, perhaps not, but we do read," he said, hastily. "And both of us might enjoy art or painting? I may not have the skill to paint anything particularly well but I have read about a new exhibition in France recently, showing the work of the great Antoine Watteau."

A sharp glance towards him from Lady Alice told Matthew that he was making no progress with the lady whatsoever.

"I do not know who Watteau might be," she informed him, firmly. "I do not think that any young lady in all of London would have such knowledge! What need is there for them to know of an artist in France?"

"He is – " Matthew snapped his mouth closed, having been about to tell her that Antoine Watteau was no longer living but then quickly realizing that the lady would have no interest in that. "Well, reading, then? What is something that you have read recently?"

Lady Alice rolled her eyes. "Only a novel, Lord Downfield, though I am sure that you would not think highly of it." She sounded bored, as though every word from him was nothing but dullness. Fear settled in Matthew's heart and he continued on regardless, striving ahead as best he could.

"I myself have only just finished reading the eighteenth section of Henry Fielding's novel."

At this, Lady Alice's eyebrows shot towards her hairline and she turned to look at him more fully, her eyes rounding. "You have read of Tom Jones?"

"I have." Relief began to chase away Matthew's fear as he smiled, seeing a new light coming into Lady Alice's eyes. "I found it a most interesting novel, though I was astonished that there were eighteen parts to it! That was very interesting. I do not often read novels but on this occasion, I did so."

"You must have enjoyed it, given that there were so many parts and you read it without giving up on the story as so many others have done," Lady Alice exclaimed, her whole expression altered now. "It is meant to become very famous, I hear, though I do think that you are the only gentleman of my acquaintance who has read each part." She tilted her head, her eyes narrowing just a fraction. "I must hope that you are telling me the truth, Lord Downfield, and not stating such a thing in the hope of pleasing me."

"I am not, I assure you! In fact, why do you not ask me some questions about the novel and I shall answer them as best as I can. Would that please you? Would it convince you that I am just as I have said?"

"I suppose that it would," Lady Alice answered, quickly, her arms folding over her chest. "Now, let me begin."

*

"You appear to have done an excellent job in convincing Lady Alice that you are one of the most excellent gentlemen in all of London!"

Matthew chuckled, elbowing Lord Dover. "I am not certain about that but at least she is no longer disinterested and frowning! I confess that I was greatly concerned that she would continue to speak of me with disregard in front of everyone else and that the *ton* would hear of it!"

"Though that does not matter, I am sure," Lord Dover answered, quickly, as they made their way through the crowd of guests. "It is only *her* opinion that matters, does it not? Especially if you are to seek to court her."

"Court her?" Matthew repeated, shaking his head. "Goodness, I certainly have no intention of doing any such thing! I have no interest in the lady in that regard."

"No?"

Matthew shook his head again. "No, of course not. You came to find me because you know how much my reputation means to me and how much of an influence Lady Alice and her mother, the Duchess, can have on society, did you not?"

Lord Dover shrugged. "Well yes, of course, but as I watched your interaction with her, as I saw the determination in your expression and your obvious delight when she began to speak with you, I presumed that there was something else – something more – on your mind. Are you telling me now that I am wrong?"

"Yes, of course I am! You are utterly mistaken!"

Lord Dover frowned. "Oh."

"The reason I put so much effort into our conversation, into hoping that she thinks well of me is simply because I wanted to make certain that my reputation is lifted all the higher in the *ton*. With what happened with Lady Sarah and knowing that some would have spoken ill of me in that regard, it is very important to me to have my reputation fully restored."

"And Lady Alice is the one who can do that."

"Who can aid it, certainly. If she thinks well of me – if I am favoured – then I am favoured with the Duke and

Duchess also. That is an excellent position to be in."

"I see." Lord Dover shrugged. "Well, all the same, I am glad the conversation went well. I was also glad to be able to pull you from Lady Sarah's company, given the difficulty that you have with her at present! No doubt you were filled with relief there."

Matthew blinked, his chest tightening. "I – I would not say – "

"There is something strange about her, I must say," Lord Dover continued, rubbing one hand over his chin. "I do not know what it is but given the extent of her knowledge in things such as art and literature, I do begin to wonder if she is a bluestocking."

Frowning, Matthew cut through the space between them with his hand. "There is no need to consider any such thing. It is quite normal for every young lady to have an interest in reading and in art."

"Ah, but this last one, the one with Antoine Watteau – and yes, Lord Rutherford told me of it in case you are wondering – seems a little odd. I did not know of such a thing and I am a gentleman who has been to France on more than one occasion! I did not even know he was an artist!"

"I did," Matthew emphasized, "and I do not think that it means that she is a bluestocking." He scowled as Lord Dover's brows furrowed. "Even if she is, what should that mean to me? There is nothing about that which would cause me any concern."

"Though if the *ton* discovered that you were often in company with a bluestocking, then many a thing might be said," Lord Dover suggested, warning running through his tone. "For a lady to be a bluestocking is a shameful thing indeed for what business do ladies have in learning the same things as gentlemen? It is not as though they *need* to be learned in any such matters and to attempt to join in conversation and discussion with gentlemen about these things ought to be an embarrassment to any young lady who tries to do so."

In an instant, Matthew recalled how Lady Sarah had spoken of crop rotation, a system which he would only expect gentlemen to know about, given that they were in charge of an estate and the business dealings there. Why would a young lady such as she have an interest in such a thing? Indeed, why would she even know the phrase, 'crop rotation'?

Could she be a bluestocking? Matthew's heart leapt up in his chest. *And if she is, then I must be careful. Lord Dover's warnings are quite right.*

"Good evening, gentlemen. I do hope that I am not intruding on any serious conversation?"

Matthew lifted his gaze and looked directly at Lord Rutherford. "Good evening, Lord Rutherford." He took in his friend's rather serious expression, seeing no smile on his face. "Is there something the matter?"

Lord Rutherford looked directly to Lord Dover and, much to Matthew's surprise, spoke with a great firmness. "Might you excuse us for a few moments, Lord Dover? I have something I wish to say to Lord Downfield which should not be said in company."

Matthew glanced to Lord Dover and then looked back again to Lord Rutherford, catching both Lord Dover's astonished expression and Lord Rutherford's set expression. He was not certain what it was that his friend wished to say but clearly, there was something of great concern on his friend's mind.

"But of course," Lord Dover murmured, frowning before he stepped away. Matthew cleared his throat, looking again to his friend and instantly, Lord Rutherford took a step closer and hissed his question in a low, dark voice.

"Whatever is it that you think you are doing?"

"Doing?" Matthew frowned. "I do not know what you mean."

"I have only just come back from dancing with Lady Catherine and she *immediately* went to Lady Sarah who was, I must say, looking rather despondent. Whatever is it that you did?"

Matthew scowled darkly. "Whyever should you think that *I* am responsible? It could very easily be that someone else had been speaking with her or upset her in some way."

Lord Rutherford poked one finger into Matthew's chest, hard. "I know because I *asked* Lady Catherine what had happened – Lady Sarah had gone to dance with Lord Donnington – and she told me that you had simply walked away from Lady Sarah without even a word of goodbye! I do not know what it is that you thought you were doing but, given our previous conversations, I had assumed that you were not only learning from all that has gone on between Lady Sarah and yourself but that you yourself were a little taken with the lady! How could you show such inconsideration?"

"I... " Try as he might, Matthew's words failed him as the heavy weight of what he had done began to sink down upon him. The more he thought about what Lord Rutherford had said, the more he realized that yes, he *had* stepped away from Lady Sarah in a rather hasty manner – and what was worse, he had not given her a single word of farewell.

"You admit to it, then?"

"It was done without thinking," Matthew stammered, aware that he now sounded foolish. "I did not mean to ignore the lady. We were having an excellent conversation, in fact and I – "

"Which surely makes it all the worse!" Lord Rutherford exclaimed, throwing up his hands. "You were in the midst of a conversation with Lady Sarah, enjoying her company and thereafter, stepped away without even saying a word to her? I cannot imagine what would have possessed you to be so inconsiderate! You, who is so careful and concerned about his reputation would then go on to treat Lady Sarah as though she has no value whatsoever?"

"It was *because* of my reputation that I stepped away!" Matthew exclaimed, embarrassment flooding him as he saw his friend's disbelieving expression. "Lord Dover came to inform me that Lady Alice and her mother – the Duchess of Kettering – were loudly discussing the gentlemen of London and thus, I *had* to step away."

His friend closed his eyes and shook his head, before pinching the bridge of his nose. "No, Downfield, you did not."

"Yes, I did," Matthew stated, stoutly. "After all that has taken place with Lady Sarah, I know that my reputation has become a little tainted. I was concerned that my standing upon her foot and then railing at her would have those in London speaking ill of me and Lady Alice was, therefore, the perfect young lady to redeem me there."

Lord Rutherford dropped his hand back to his side and then stared back at Matthew as though he could not quite believe what he was hearing. "So you used Lady Alice for your own gains?"

Matthew blinked rapidly, shock beginning to spread out across his chest. "No, I did not *use* her. Instead, I had conversation with the lady and we spoke at length about a good many things. It took some time for me to encourage her to speak, however, for she was a little reluctant and indeed, had even forgotten that we had already been acquainted!

Once we found something to discuss, then all was quite well. I was pleased with our conversation, for though I had attempted to speak of art, she knew nothing of it but when I mentioned Henry Fielding, then everything improved in a moment!"

"And do you intend to continue this connection?"

Matthew shrugged. "Mayhap. I do not have any concern when it comes to continuing speaking with her on occasion. I am glad that she thinks well of me and that the *ton* will, no doubt, soon hear of it."

"So that I understand, let me speak this clearly to you," Lord Rutherford said, just as Matthew finished speaking, his eyebrows falling low over his eyes and sending shadows there. "You heard of Lady Alice and her mother discussing the gentlemen of London and their merits and, without thought nor consideration for Lady Sarah, the lady whose company you had been enjoying, you hurried away. Thereafter, you used the knowledge that you have gained *solely* through your conversation with Lady Sarah to then improve yourself upon Lady Alice and, no doubt, not mentioning her once at all but instead making it appear as though everything that you said came from your own knowledge and interests. You have no interest in the lady herself, have no intention of pursuing a further connection with Lady Alice but were only using the conversation with her – and her interest in you – so that both she and her mother will speak well of you and talk to their friends and acquaintances about you. Your status and standing in society will be lifted and restored, just as you please, and this, to your mind, means that all is well."

Matthew swallowed hard, hearing everything that Lord Rutherford had said and sensing with it, a slow burning guilt beginning to wash over him. "Yes, that is just as it is," he said, firmly, refusing to let the guilt wash over him. "I do not see why – "

"The truth is, you *do* see why there is difficulty there," Lord Rutherford interjected, throwing up his hands. "You can see it, you can feel it and yet your sense of pride and your determination to elevate yourself covers over it all."

"That is a trifle unfair," Matthew complained, as his friend shook his head. "I – I do not have more pride than any other gentleman."

"That is nonsense. You are the most prideful, arrogant gentleman that I know and I say this without any malice or unkindness meant." Lord Rutherford spoke quietly still but his words were like hammer blows, hitting hard against Matthew's heart. "This is why I did not aid you when it came to Lady Sarah's little mysteries, for I could see the benefit of what she was forcing upon you and, for a time, I thought that there was a great effect coming over you. Now, however, I see that there is nothing that can take you away from yourself, from your own desires and considerations." He took another step closer, his eyes blazing. "Did you even think for a moment of what Lady Sarah would feel when you stepped away from her like that? Did that ever come into your thoughts or did you not even think of her for a single moment?"

Matthew closed his eyes, refusing to say a single word to his friend for fear that, if he did so, the guilt which pressed down heavily upon him would break apart and envelop him entirely. No, he realized, he had not thought for a second what his actions would do to Lady Sarah. He had not given her a moment, had been so eager to step away and speak to Lady Alice that he had forgotten about her in a moment.

"Ask yourself this, my friend," Lord Rutherford finished, putting one hand on Matthew's shoulder as though to soften the harshness of his words. "In which lady's company would you prefer to linger?" When Matthew looked at him, Lord Rutherford dropped his hand and shrugged. "Would you prefer to be in Lady Alice's company, knowing that everything you do and say is being judged and fearing that if you do not engage her in conversation, if you do not *please* her, then she might speak ill of you? Or would you prefer to speak with Lady Sarah, knowing that you enjoy her conversation, that you are treated with kindness and consideration, despite all that you have done?"

He did not give Matthew a chance to answer but stepped away, leaving a weight settling over Matthew's heart which he could not dislodge. He tried to tell himself that all was well, that he had done nothing wrong but the words that his friend had spoken to him and the guilt which now encased him would not permit him to do so.

I did not think of her for even a moment, he realized, rubbing one hand over his eyes for a moment. *All I thought of was myself.*

The truth was, in the scenario that Lord Rutherford had set out, Matthew knew in an instant which lady he would prefer to be seen with, which he would prefer to spend time with. It was not even a thought to him, for Lady Sarah's company was far more preferable than that of Lady Alice's! He had only gone to speak with the latter because of what she might be able to do for his standing but had found the conversation a little flat and lackluster... whereas with Lady Sarah, he enjoyed every moment of her company.

So why, then, did I treat her with such inconsideration?

The truth of it rang so furiously around him that Matthew could not breathe for a moment. He had never once wanted to admit that he was prideful, had never once believed that he had any more arrogance than any other fellow but now, as he considered all that had taken place, he realized the truth.

He was nothing more than a gentleman filled with thoughts about his own self; pride wrapped around him like a coat – a coat that he wore willingly and decorated in bright colors. He loved the feeling of being known, the sensation of being noticed and, that selfishness had now gone on to injure Lady Sarah most severely.

Matthew swallowed tightly, his jaw fixing hard. He ought to go at once and beg for her to forgive him, to apologise for what he had done, but the thought of doing so was not a pleasant one. Instead, with his head dropped low, Matthew made his way to the card room rather than linger in the ballroom, finding his spirits sinking all the heavier with every step he took. He had ruined Lady Sarah's evening, no doubt, had made their own connection a little strained and had come to recognize just how much of a fool he was.

There was very little left for him here.

Chapter Eleven

Sarah picked up a ribbon and then set it back down without so much as looking at it. She ran her finger lightly down over the silk but then turned away, her heart holding no interest in the fripperies around her.

"Have you found anything you like?"

With a shake of her head, Sarah offered Lady Catherine a small smile. "No, not as yet."

Lady Catherine tilted her head. "You are not in fine spirits this afternoon, are you? Whatever is the trouble?"

Sarah paused for a moment, considering, then sighed. "It is foolishness, of course, by my thoughts still linger on the ball."

"The one three nights ago?"

With a nod, Sarah looked away, feeling a tingling heat in her cheeks. "It is only that he turned his back on me so hastily, I was left feeling worthless – almost foolish – in his eyes, though I know that I am not so."

"No, you are not!" Lady Catherine exclaimed, reaching out to grasp Sarah's hand and squeeze it tightly. "My dear friend, you are delightful. You have a great deal of worth, even if Lord Downfield does not see it." Her eyes searched Sarah's face. "Though I must wonder if there is some reason that you hope for him to see you in that way? It seems that rather than simply ignoring his lack of consideration and reminding yourself of how selfish and arrogant he can be, you have really taken this to heart. It seems as though you are injured by it in a way that I did not expect."

"I did not expect it either," Sarah admitted, quietly. "My dear Catherine, it is nonsense to let myself behave so, I am well aware of that, but my heart simply will not release that moment from my thoughts! I am sorrowful over it. I am *injured* by it, as you have said, and I cannot seem to forget it."

"Because you care for him."

Sarah blinked rapidly, putting one hand to her heart. "Care for him? Indeed not, I hardly think that I would ever permit myself to be so foolish!"

"You are drawn to him, then."

Again, Sarah tried to find the words to refute this, only for them to stick in her throat. She could say nothing, fighting to find the right words to say though none of them came.

"It is quite all right to find yourself drawn to a gentleman, no matter how unexpected that may be," Lady Catherine told her, as Sarah threw a hasty glance around the shop, hoping that no-one else had overheard their conversation. "Lord Rutherford and I have found ourselves that way, I confess, and that has been most surprising! I did not think for a moment that one simple introduction would cause my heart to act in the way that it has but… " She shrugged and smiled. "I cannot pretend that it has not."

"Just as I cannot pretend that there is nothing within my heart for Lord Downfield," Sarah sighed, heavily. "I do wish that I felt nothing more than dislike for him, for that would be a good deal easier, would it not?"

"No, I do not think so. This is not something that you should hide, not even from yourself," Lady Catherine said, quickly. "Do not think that I am at all surprised, nor will I encourage you to do all you can to forget the fellow! No, instead, I will tell you simply to permit yourself to feel all that you feel without any great concern. Do not continually think on it or pretend that there is nothing there. Rather, let it be as it will be and the path will soon make itself clear."

Sarah frowned. "My dear friend, it sounds as though

that you think that my current feelings may grow! I cannot tell you how much I pray that they do quite the opposite."

"But why?"

"Because I do not *want* to feel anything for him," Sarah answered, spreading out her hands. "I do not want to have even the smallest interest in him. Look how he treated me! Look how foolish I am now, to have such feelings pressed back at me as though I mean nothing." Her eyes closed tightly, heat burning behind them. "I *am* nothing to him. That was made very clear and it is foolishness now to permit even the smallest flicker of interest to remain in my heart."

Lady Catherine opened her mouth and then closed it again, a frown flickering there. She shook her head, then tried to speak again but all that came out was a sigh.

"You see?" Sarah murmured, softly. "Even you can see that what I have said makes sense. Lord Downfield may have begun to learn something about his character but it will not make a profound difference to him. I have understood that now."

"Mayhap. Though I will not fully agree with you," Lady Catherine said, firmly. "Come now, if you are not going to purchase anything then why do we not take our leave?" Her eyes twinkled suddenly. "We might step into the bookshop?"

A thrill ran up Sarah's spine. "Do you think we might?"

"We have not managed to do so as yet and since we are without parent to guard us this afternoon, I can see no reason why not."

Sarah beamed at her friend, her concern and her thoughts over Lord Downfield quickly fading. She stepped outside quickly and, with hurried steps made her way towards the bookshop. With a hasty glance all around her, she made her way into the shop with Lady Catherine following close behind.

The moment she stepped into the shop, Sarah's face split with a smile. The aura of books filled the space, the scent of pages and ink rushing over her. It warmed her heart and, after so long being absent from her favorite place, Sarah let out a long, contented sigh and clasped her hands tight together.

Lady Catherine laughed softly. "We shall have to take great care not to stay too long," she warned, as Sarah nodded. "Your mother and mine are expecting us to return within the hour and we cannot be tardy. Though, if there are any books that you wish to purchase, then I shall keep them safe at my townhouse and, should you wish to come to take tea with me one afternoon, we might spend a pleasant afternoon indulging in whatever we have purchased!"

"A wonderful idea," Sarah breathed, beginning to make her way to the rows of books. "I think I shall be quite lost here for some time!" Her fingertips drifted along the row of books, brushing gently across every spine. With a smile, she picked one up, opened up to the first page and began to read. Within minutes, she was lost.

***

"Good afternoon, Lady Sarah."

With a yelp of surprise, Sarah lifted her head and managed to drop the book at the very same time. Lord Downfield's eyebrows lifted in surprise though he quickly reached down to pick up the book and hand it back to her, though he glanced at the cover as he did so.

"Goodness, Lady Sarah, I did not think that a young lady such as yourself would be so interested in the history of the world. I would have thought that knowing the Kings and Queens of England would be the most that any young lady would be required to recall!"

Sarah snapped the book shut and then placed it on the shelf, the fright he had given her beginning to rush through her frame, her heart clamoring. "I am interested in a good many things, Lord Downfield. History of any country is something that I find myself truly fascinated by." Realizing that, yet again, she had spoken without thinking and revealed a little more of her tendencies towards learning and the like, Sarah flushed and shrugged. "Though I am also partial to an interesting novel also, of course."

"Mmm." Lord Downfield tilted his head. "Though you prefer to expand your mind, I think."

Sarah blinked, not quite certain what to say.

"Should you like me to purchase this book for you? It would be my pleasure to do so."

Shaking her head quickly, Sarah took a step back. "I thank you, but no."

"No? Are you quite sure? You appeared to be engrossed in it when I arrived, though I confess I did not mean to startle you."

Sarah swallowed at a sudden tightness in her throat, shaking her head as she did so. "You are very kind, Lord Downfield, but I am afraid that I cannot accept such a gift."

He came closer to her, his eyes a little grave now. "This is because of what I did at the ball, is it not? You are no longer willing to consider me anything more than a mere acquaintance? I cannot blame you for that, of course – and indeed, I do not – but I should very much like to express my regret to you for how I behaved. It was foolishness on my part – nay, more than that, it was selfishness." He drew himself up as surprise lodged in Sarah's heart, sending a stillness over her. "It was utter selfishness, Lady Sarah. I can admit to that now, though I was not at all inclined to do so when Lord Rutherford spoke to me about it all. However, I am grateful for it because it made me realize that the disregard with which I had treated you was deeply inconsiderate and for that I am truly sorry. Indeed, I should never have even *thought* to step away and even though I spoke to Lady Alice at length, I found that my only desire for conversation was with you."

A little overcome with all that had been said to her and the rush with which those words had been spoken, Sarah took a few moments to gain her composure as she stood as tall as she could and looked Lord Downfield directly in the eye. It was quite astonishing to hear him speak with such honesty but the look on his face and the fervency with which he had spoken made her believe that he was quite genuine. "Might I ask why it was that you abandoned me, Lord Downfield? From what I could see, it was so that you could speak to another young lady and her mother which I could understand, if you were interested in courting her?"

At this, Lord Downfield cleared his throat, dropped his head and shuffled his feet, pink beginning to rise in his cheeks. "No, I can assure you that I have no interest in doing such a thing."

Relief swelled in Sarah's heart but she pushed it back as quickly as she could. "I see. Then what was your purpose in rushing towards this young lady as you did?"

Lord Downfield coughed and raked one hand over his hair, his eyes now darting away from her. "It was all to improve my own standing, that is all. It is unimportant for it was nothing but selfish and I can see that now. I regret it all the more, recognising that it brought you pain and upset."

"I understand," Sarah murmured, her heart quickening as she realized just how much he meant every word. "I do appreciate your apology, Lord Downfield, I – "

She stopped suddenly as Lady Catherine came hurrying towards them both, her eyes wide. She did not even stop to greet Lord Downfield but grasped Sarah's arm.

"Your mother and mine have just driven past in the carriage," she hissed, as Sarah's heart began to slam furiously about her chest. "I did not think that they were coming into town and it is only good fortune that let me see them for I was looking out of the window at the time – but we must take our leave."

"Of course." Sarah looked up at Lord Downfield, seeing him frown. "Forgive me, Lord Downfield, but I must hurry away from you now. I beg your forgiveness."

"But the third mystery!" Lord Downfield exclaimed, his hand now catching hers. "You must tell me the third mystery that you were to offer me. I want to begin it just as soon as I can."

"I will write to you with it," Sarah said hurriedly, pressing his fingers. "I must go. Forgive me, I *must* go. I cannot be seen here."

Without another word to him, she wrenched her hand away from his and then hurried after Lady Catherine, whose face had gone very pale indeed.

"Wait a moment." Lady Catherine pushed open the door very carefully and then stepped outside, letting herself walk forward into the sunshine and looking all about her. Sarah, her heart pounding, waited just inside the shop only for Lady Catherine to nod. Yanking open the door with all of her strength, she stepped out quickly and then both she and Lady Catherine walked away from the bookshop as fast as they could.

"We have been to the milliner's already but mayhap we should step inside again?" Sarah suggested, as Lady Catherine nodded. "Thank you for the warning. I do not know what would have happened should my mother have seen me stepping out of the bookshop!"

"I quite understand. It is a blessing that I saw them when I did!" Lady Catherine exclaimed as they made their way back into the milliner's. "Lord Downfield did look very confused but I am sure that you can come up with some excuse should he bring it up."

"I must hope so," Sarah murmured, biting her lip as she recalled the confused expression on Lord Downfield's face. "Though quite what it shall be, I have very little idea."

Chapter Twelve

How very curious.

"Are you ready, Downfield?"

Matthew started slightly as the gentleman to his left nudged him. "Yes, of course. Forgive me." He quickly pulled out one of his cards and placed it down on the table.

"You have not drawn yet!" the gentleman exclaimed, as Lord Rutherford, sitting opposite, began to chuckle. "*Take a card and then discard one!*"

"Of course." Embarrassed, Matthew took a card from the top of the pile. "I shall not make the same mistake again, I am sure. Forgive me."

Lord Rutherford grinned but Matthew scowled, a little frustrated that he had been so distracted in his thoughts so as to miss his turn at cards. The game continued and Matthew did his utmost to concentrate, telling himself that he was to do nothing other than simply play but time and again, his mind filled with thoughts of Lady Sarah, and there seemed to be nothing he could do to stop it.

Why had she left the bookshop in such haste? If it had been any earlier, he would have assumed it was because of his presence but they had spoken, he had apologized and the conversation had been going well. Then, Lady Catherine had appeared, said something which Matthew had not overheard completely and Lady Sarah's face had drained of color. Her smile had shattered in an instant, her eyes rounding with fright and she had hurried away from him without even hesitating. When he had caught her hand and asked about the third mystery, it was not because he had any real interest in such a thing but was only eager to stay in her company for a little longer – or to know what it was that had frightened her so. Matthew had not found himself irritated but, rather, concerned.

"It is your turn again, Downfield, though you do not appear to be in the least bit interested in the game."

"That is because I am not," Matthew answered, drawing a card and then immediately discarding it. "But I shall play to this round's end and then, I think, I shall take my leave."

One of the gentlemen at the table chuckled, catching Matthew's attention. "Might it be that you are thinking of a particular young lady? I believe that you were in deep and prolonged conversation with her of late. Society has been abuzz with the news of that!"

"Has it now?" Matthew murmured, rolling his eyes in order to express utter disinclination for all that was said of him. "Those in society should know that I am very often seen in the company of young ladies. That can be no surprise to anyone, I am sure."

"But it is certainly significant that you have been the one to encourage her in conversation? That she is now clearly interested in your company and desires more of it? I should say that it is all *very* significant indeed!"

"Especially given the whispers about her."

This remark from another gentleman entirely made Matthew frown heavily. "I do not know what whispers you speak of."

"Oh, that she is inclined towards seeking a husband this Season!"

Matthew blinked rapidly, surprise coursing through him. "Seeking a husband?"

"Yes, did you not know? I was sure that everyone in the *ton* was aware of that! Though, of course, the lady might be unwilling to even consider you and then the *ton* would find that mirthful indeed, I am sure!"

Rather confused at this remark, Matthew shook his head. "I can assure you, I have no interest in matrimony this Season. Any conversations I have engaged in or any interest I have shown has been solely for my own purposes, I can assure you."

"And I would concur with that," Lord Rutherford said a little darkly, scowling as Matthew shot him a look.

"Is that so?" The gentleman who had begun the conversation tipped his head and looked long at Matthew. "And would you not say that you are in the least bit concerned as regards the lady's considerations of you? It seems to me that you might disappoint her."

Matthew hesitated, finding himself torn in two directions. He wanted to say that he did truly care for Lady Sarah and what she thought of him but neither did he want these gentlemen to know his true feelings for the lady, especially when he was not certain of them himself! "I think that she would have to be disappointed," he said eventually, catching how the other gentlemen glanced at each other. "I would never think to even *call* upon a young lady if she were to have thoughts of courtship or the like upon her mind. I am flattered by her interest in my conversation, of course, but that is all that there is to it." He caught the way that Lord Rutherford shook his head and had to force himself not to speak to him directly, not to express the confusion which, at present, still tied itself around his heart. Lord Rutherford might think ill of him, he knew, but it could not be helped, not at this moment. He would explain both to his friend *and* to Lady Sarah herself, if he had to. But for the moment, this was all he could do.

"I must say, I am surprised to hear you speak so bluntly," the second gentleman said, as Matthew looked down at the cards in his hand, trying to focus on the game rather than on what the opinion of other gentlemen might be. "I would have thought that to have the attentions of that particular young lady might give you pause... but it seems that I am wrong!"

Matthew did not understand what they spoke of, a little confused as to why they would speak so highly of Lady Sarah who, as far he was aware, was indistinct within the *ton*. With a shrug, he played the next card and the game continued. Choosing to remain silent, Matthew battled his thoughts inwardly, fighting to keep control over his tongue so that he said not even the smallest thing about either Lady Sarah or his own connection to her. All the same, he was sure he felt Lord Rutherford's eyes on him, like sharp daggers poking into his skin and, at the same time, felt the scrutiny of the other gentlemen also. When the game ended, Matthew rose to his feet and excused himself, nodding to Lord Rutherford who, after a moment, nodded in return.

"I think it is time for me to return home," Matthew said, suddenly desperate for his own company. "You will have to excuse me, gentlemen. I am sorry, but it is a late hour and I am much too weary to stay a minute longer. Do excuse me!" With that, he turned on his heel and stepped out, relieved to be out of the game and away from other company.

**

It was not until Matthew arrived home that he felt a little more at ease. Sitting back in his chair in front of a small fire that burned in the grate, he closed his eyes and let out a long breath, a glass of brandy in his hand. His whole body softened, his eyes closing as finally, all thoughts of Lady

Sarah, all confusing and conflicting emotions began to leave him.

A scratch at the door interrupted him and with a groan, Matthew called for his servant to enter.

"My lord, forgive the late interruption but there is a note here for you and it is urgent."

Matthew frowned and quickly sat up straight, reaching for the note. "Urgent, you say? Who brought it?"

"A ragamuffin child, my lord. He told me that he had already been paid and would be paid more once the answer was given to him."

"Answer?" Confused, Matthew broke open the seal and unfolded the short note. Reading the words quickly, the heaviness of his frown grew and he shook his head, his jaw tightening. Looking up at the butler, he waved one hand. "Go to the child and tell him that the answer is that yes, I shall do as is asked. That is all that is required."

The butler nodded and quit the room at once, leaving Matthew to look at the note alone. He settled back in his chair again, aware of the worry which was beginning to pour into his heart. This note from Lady Sarah was interesting, certainly, though it still brought both concern and confusion to his mind.

'Lord Downfield, I write to you with the third mystery, as I said I would do,' the note began. 'I must ask you, do you know what great Roman discovery was made of late? And by a woman no less! I do hope that this will not be too great a mystery and indeed, mayhap you have already read of this? Lastly, and this is not at all related to all that I have said before, I must beg of you not to tell a soul that you spoke with me in the bookshop. That must sound very strange and while it is, I cannot give you any further explanation than that. I do hope that you will consent to this, despite your lack *of understanding? It would bring me a great deal of relief. I will wait in the hope of your quick reply. Yours, etc.'*

"Why would she not wish for anyone to know that she was in the bookshop?" Matthew murmured aloud, frowning as he looked again at the note. It was a very strange request indeed and though Matthew was more than contented to do as she asked, he wanted to know the reason behind her asking such a thing. Was she afraid? That had certainly been the expression on her face when she had rushed from the bookshop that day – and if she was fearful, then Matthew wanted very much to assist her.

I have behaved abominably with her in the past, he reminded himself, screwing up his face at the recollection, *and treated her with a great lack of consideration. And yet now, I want to prove myself to her, to prove that I am willing to do – and to be – all that she desires in this. Somehow or other, I* will *do it.* He thumped one fist on top of the arm of the chair, the other hand still holding the note. *For her, I think I might just do anything.*

A great overwhelming sense of relief washed over him, as though he was finally admitting to himself all that he felt for the lady. It was more than just being in her company, more than just being in conversation with her now and again. There was a true desire within him, a hope that he might find himself often with her, enjoying all that she had to say and delighting in the smiles she offered him. She made him want to improve himself, and his past shames now made him all the more determined to become all the better a gentleman. How quickly he had turned away from her before! How foolish he had been to think that Lady Alice offered him more!

Matthew passed one hand over his eyes, grimacing. Those truths settled in his heart but, all the same, the worry about the *ton* and all that they thought of him still lingered there. He had not removed it from himself, not yet at least, and that concerned him a great deal.

"But I will fight it," he said to himself, aloud. "I will fight hard and fight for as long as I must endure until I conquer it." His hand thumped the arm of the chair for the second time, a fresh determination flooding his very soul. "And I will do so for her."

Chapter Thirteen

"Do you think that he will get the answer?"

Sarah smiled. "I do not know, it depends on how much he has read of late. Though I do suspect that he might well have disregarded that, even if he *had* read it, given that the discovery was made by Frances herself, rather than by her husband, Thomas Knight."

"Though I am sure that Mr. Knight himself was very pleased with his wife's discovery and her skill!"

"Indeed." Sarah let out a small sigh as she and Lady Caroline walked through St James' Park. "One does wonder what it would be like to have a husband who celebrated learning and the like, who championed achievement over pushing it aside."

Lady Catherine nudged her gently. "It may be that Lord Downfield is led to change his opinion on such things, once he is convinced that there is merit in them," she said gently, though Sarah flushed immediately, a little embarrassed that her own thoughts had become all the more apparent. "There may be understanding there. He might find himself pleased to know that you are as learned as he!"

Sarah laughed despite her embarrassment. "I hardly think that I am as learned as he! It is foolishness to think so and I would not even imagine it, given that I have not gone to Eton. My governess was excellent, of course, but all the same – "

"But why could it not be?" Lady Catherine asked, challenging Sarah gently. "You have loved to learn, reading all that you can and, thus far, proving to Lord Downfield that he is *not* as well informed as she! That can be no bad thing, surely? I do not see it as such, though he might well do!"

Sarah laughed again, her face still flushed but her spirits lifting. "I shall have to wait and see if he *ever* speaks of that in a positive manner," she said, though her smile began to quickly fade away. "I confess, it has been a disappointment to my heart that my parents are so determined to quash such a thing. I thought that they might... well, I thought that it would be seen as a good thing, that it would enhance the qualities they are so eager to show to the gentlemen of London but instead, I have received entirely the opposite response."

Lady Catherine smiled sadly and looped her arm through Sarah's. "Mayhap whatever husband you end up finding shall be just the opposite," she said, firmly. "I have hope for that. After all, Lord Rutherford has no concerns whatsoever about the many books I have read and the many books I hope to read! I am sure there will be other gentlemen – whether it is Lord Downfield or not – who feel the very same way." She smiled and Sarah made to say more, only for Lady Catherine's eyes to flare wide, her face split with a smile as she waved eagerly, bringing their walk to a stop. "Look, Lord Rutherford is present now! Can you see him? He is coming towards us now, look how happy he is to see me!" She squeezed Sarah's arm and Sarah smiled, glad that her friend had found such happiness with Lord Rutherford. Lady Catherine had informed her only a few minutes earlier, before their conversation about Lord Downfield, that Lord Rutherford had sought to court her and that her father had consented. It seemed that all was well for Lady Catherine and Sarah was delighted for her.

"Oh, he brings Lord Downfield with him!" Lady Catherine exclaimed, as Sarah's heart immediately leapt up in surprise. "See? He comes to join Lord Rutherford very quickly indeed!"

Sarah watched as a gentleman detached himself from a small gathered crowd and, coming to join Lord Rutherford, came directly towards them both. Her heart began to quicken, a sense of anticipation – and a little anxiety – beginning to worry her. She did not know what he would have made of the note that she had sent him and seeing him now, face to face, made her feel a little uncertain. Would he question her as to why she had asked him such a strange thing? Or would he stay silent?

From the moment that Lord Downfield came to join them, Sarah knew that he was thinking about her note. The questions in his eyes were many, his lips a little flatter than usual as if he were pressing them hard, in order not to demand answers to them. He bowed and Sarah bobbed a curtsy, making sure to greet them both.

"You will think me very rude, Lady Sarah, I am sure, but I must walk with Lady Catherine for a time." Lord Rutherford beamed at Lady Catherine rather than looking to Sarah at all, though she smiled her consent, just as Lady Catherine dropped her hand from her arm.

"But of course, I quite understand."

"And might I, then, be permitted to walk with you?" Lord Downfield smiled but it did not bring any sort of light to his eyes. "Even if it is only for a short while, I should be very glad to be in your company again."

Sarah swallowed at the tightness which had immediately come into her throat. "But of course," she said again, a little embarrassed that she had spoken the very same words to him as she had said to Lord Rutherford. "I do hope that all is well with you, Lord Downfield?" She tried to keep her voice light. "Am I to hope that you have the answer for me already?"

Lord Downfield chuckled dryly and Sarah relaxed just a

little as she took his arm. "No, I have not. I should tell you, however, that I spend some of last evening doing some reading and then again this morning but, as yet, I have found nothing of note. I am sure that someone will know of it, however."

"Many people know of it," Lord Rutherford said, turning his head back to speak directly to Lord Downfield, his grin already bright. "It is just that *you* have not read of it and therefore, you are entirely unaware of whom this lady speaks! I, on the other hand, am well aware of the discovery and think it a very excellent thing. I should like to learn more about it, I think."

Sarah smiled back at him and when she looked to Lord Downfield, found herself relieved that he was grinning back at Lord Rutherford rather than being at all irritated that his friend knew of this when he did not.

"You have given me a clue, at least, for it is surprising to hear that a woman made this discovery," Lord Downfield continued, making Sarah's smile slip a little. "Though mayhap I should not judge that. After all, though it is unusual, it should not be ignored, should it? I have heard that there has even been a woman giving lectures of late, though that is not something that I have had any interest in attending… not because it was a woman, you understand, but simply because the topic did not interest me."

A little delighted to hear this, Sarah's smile returned quickly. "I think you mean Charlotte Murchinson? She has been giving lectures in the King's College, on geology I believe." Seeing his eyebrows lift, Sarah's smile grew all the more. "Though even if you were interested in attending, you would not have been permitted to do so as it has only been to other ladies that she has been permitted to speak."

"Ah." Lord Downfield did not make any remark in that

regard, did not say as to whether he considered that a right practice. Instead, he frowned and Sarah found herself smiling, glad that he was not rejecting the idea at least. Perhaps what Lady Catherine had said in giving her hope about Lord Downfield was correct.

"You champion the ladies who make great strides in certain fields, do you not?" Lord Downfield asked, turning his head to look at her. "I do think that a good thing, Lady Sarah."

"Do you?" Sarah asked, a little surprised. "I would have thought the opposite."

"Would you?" Lord Downfield smiled a little lightly, his lips twisting. "Well, I can understand that, I suppose. A gentleman such as I, who has done nothing but speak of myself, who has pushed myself to the fore, who has done nothing but think only of my own standing in society... yes, I can quite understand why you would think so."

"I did not mean any insult," Sarah said hastily, only for Lord Downfield to smile and quickly shake his head.

"Do not think that I mean to upset you in any way," he answered, as she gazed back into his eyes, the worry she had felt beginning to pull away from her now. "You have made me reflect upon myself a great deal. That very first mystery you gave me, the very first trial I was offered as regarded Tom Jones brought me anger, frustration and upset... and then I realised just how foolish and selfish I had become. I was angry at being forced to do so – though of course, I see now that I was not forced at all, not by your hand – and thereafter, irritated that I would have to waste time reading a nonsensical book! I felt myself shamed when I realised that I did not know something which you already did and that brought me to a prolonged period of reflection. For all of it, Lady Sarah, I confess that I am glad though I certainly have not always been so!"

"No, indeed you have not been!" Sarah exclaimed, only to blush furiously as Lord Downfield shot her a quick look. She squeezed her eyes closed but after a moment, a bark of laughter from Lord Downfield shattered her embarrassment and, opening her eyes, she saw him grinning at her. The light in his eyes, the joy in his expression and the warm, broad smile made her feel as though she was truly accepted, truly known – and that nothing she had said or might say would ever be taken badly. How different he was to the gentleman she had known him to be! How strange that he would be so altered now! Though, Sarah considered, as she too let herself laugh, how much she appreciated that change.

"I do appreciate your honesty, Lady Sarah, more than you might know," Lord Downfield said, with a chuckle. "You are also very forgiving, given my past mistakes and ill treatment of you." His smile softened and the look in his eyes became almost tender. "I do not think that I know any young lady who would have shown such grace. You are quite marvelous, I think."

Sarah did not know what to say to this,. She turned her gaze away from him, the heat back in her face though this time, it came from a sense of delight rather than from any sort of embarrassment. Warmth curled in her stomach and her lips curved upwards as she darted another glance towards him, seeing that same softness about his eyes.

Whatever was happening to her? What was happening between them? She could not quite understand it and yet, found herself desiring even more of whatever this could be.

"You have also been very understanding, Lord Downfield," she said, choosing now to bring up the note she had written to him simply so that it would not be sitting on the edge of her thoughts. "When I wrote to you with that very strange request, your response could not have come more quickly and it did bring me a great deal of relief."

"But of course." Lord Downfield leaned a little closer to her, her hand still on his arm. "Though," he continued, his voice dropping low, "if there is something that you are having difficulty with, I would be glad to aid you where I can."

She looked back at him, a little surprised. "Truly?"

He nodded, his expression now one of concern as his eyes searched her face. "I believe that you are afraid of something, Lady Sarah, are you not? I do not know what it is nor do I understand why you had to rush away from the bookshop with such haste but I confess that I do not much like seeing you so. It worries me that there is such a fear in your heart. I do not want to pry either, however, but if there is anything that I might do in order to relieve your fears in some way, then I would be glad to do it."

Sarah's throat closed up as tears burned behind her eyes. She was not upset over his words but rather so touched by his consideration and kindness that she did not know what to say.

"I hope I have not upset you!" Lord Downfield exclaimed, only for Sarah to laugh and shake her head, reaching across so she might pat his hand with hers.

"No, indeed you have not, I assure you. It is only that I have never had anyone speak so kindly to me, aside from Lady Catherine. She is the only one who knows of my present struggles and I very much appreciate her consideration, as I do yours. Though, at the present moment, there is not much I wish to tell you, simply because to explain it would take a prolonged length of time – and a discussion thereafter, mayhap, and I do not think that either of us have the time for such a thing!"

"I think you are mistaken there, Lady Sarah. I should be very glad to listen to you for however long it should take.

Believe me, there is nothing I should like better."

Sarah's heart swelled all the more and for a moment, she swayed in her decision to remain silent and keep her explanation to herself. She wanted to tell him all, to explain to him why she had rushed from the bookshop, why her mother and father had prevented her from keeping even a single book in the house.

But then the thought of telling him and what that might mean for their connection flew over her and inwardly, a twist of fear caught her heart and she shook her head. "I am quite sure it is not an explanation I need to give you at present but I am truly grateful to you for your consideration and for your concern."

Lord Downfield's face fell and he let out a heavy breath, as if a little disappointed by her decision not to speak. "Very well. But you must promise me that, should you ever find yourself in need of a confidante, of someone willing and eager to listen and to help you in whatever way you need, you will come to me." He stopped and turned to face her, her hand slipping from his arm for a moment. "Please, Lady Sarah. Do come to me should you require anything. I should like to be a support to you in whatever way I can."

Sarah looked back at him and felt her heart squeeze with a painful awareness of just how much she wanted to lean forward and rest in his arms. She wanted to feel his arms around her waist, wanted to breathe him in as she closed her eyes and rested her face on his shoulder.

Whatever was wrong with her? One did not think such things about a gentleman! And yet, as Sarah watched him, her heart's yearning grew all the more rather than fading. She could not find what to say, did not know what it was she ought to respond to but instead, simply put one hand to her heart and then closed her eyes for just a moment.

"You can trust me, Sarah."

Opening her eyes, she gazed back at him. "Yes, Lord Downfield, I believe that I can," she said, softly. "I promise you that, should I require your aid in any way, I shall tell you at once."

"Good."

"I suppose that we should return now, Sarah."

Sarah turned her head to see Lady Catherine and Lord Rutherford coming to join them., though there was a knowing smile on Lady Catherine's face. Blushing, Sarah pulled her hand from Lord Downfield's arm again, where she had only just placed it. "Yes, I suppose that we should. It will soon be time for us to prepare for this evening." She turned and dropped into a quick curtsy, suddenly eager to escape from him simply so that she might not lose her composure completely in front of him. It was clear that Lady Catherine was aware of what Sarah herself was feeling given the smile on her face, and Sarah did not want to permit her friend time to make any sort of comment about it, not while they were in company. "Good afternoon, Lord Downfield. Thank you for our walk. I enjoyed our conversation."

Much to her astonishment, Lord Downfield reached out, caught her hand and after a moment, bent over it. His lips whispered across the back of her hand, though he did not kiss it, but the heat of his breath was enough to make her tremble.

"I enjoyed every moment," he told her, quietly enough for Lady Catherine and Lord Rutherford not to hear him. "Please, remember what I said."

She nodded. "I shall."

The gentlemen both stepped away and quickly, Lady Catherine caught Sarah's arm and pulled close to Sarah. "So what was said between the two of you? When Lord

Rutherford turned to return me to you, we both noticed how intensely he was speaking to you. I do hope all has gone well?"

Sarah nodded. "It has."

"And does he know the answer to your third mystery?"

With a laugh, Sarah shook her head. "Indeed not, though he is not as against that question as I thought! I feared that he might dislike hearing that there was a lady involved in such a thing, but he has not made any remark in that regard."

"Eager for your company also, yes?"

Sarah laughed and shook her head. "I do not think so but he is certainly improved, that is something I am quite certain about."

"Indeed, even Lord Rutherford has noticed it, though he seemed a little irritated about something – I am not sure as to what for he did not speak of it entirely. But that does not matter, I am sure, so long as you are contented!"

Sarah considered this and then found herself smiling, her heart lifting with a sense of happiness which she had never before felt. "I am happy," she said, softly. "Very happy indeed."

Chapter Fourteen

Matthew strode into the ballroom, his heart filled with an expectation that he could not remove. It threaded through his veins, sending an anticipation and an excitement there and Matthew could not help but smile. It was not in greeting to those he passed, it was not in happy expectation of the dancing that might follow. No, all of his thoughts and the only reason for his happiness lay in Lady Sarah's presence. Very soon, he would see her again, very soon he would be in her company and that was all that Matthew could think about. Mayhap she would dance with him, mayhap she would accept his desire to have her in his arms – and if she did, then Matthew's delight would be never ending. The answer to her mysteries seemed no longer of any importance, the frustration he had once felt gone completely. His only desire was to be near to her, to talk with her, to laugh with her, to enjoy her company, to let his eyes fill with her beauty.

And this evening, Matthew intended to tell her.

"Good evening, Downfield!"

Matthew's smile dropped. "Lord Stephenson, good evening. How are you?"

"Very well." He looked around the room. "There is certainly something of a crush here this evening, is there not?"

"There is, though that is not a bad thing. I usually find myself quite delighted to be in the company of so many fine young ladies, though I am sure that there are some that you are more eagerly looking forward to seeing than others!"

At this, Matthew shot him a sharp look, his brows furrowing. He waited for a moment to see if Lord Stephenson would explain but his friend did not. Instead, he offered Matthew a knowing smile, as though he was somehow meant to know what was meant.

Matthew cleared his throat. "You are to have your night filled with dances, I am sure."

"Of course I shall!" Lord Stephenson chuckled, only for Lord Dover to come to join them. "You know very well that I have a great many acquaintances and there are so many that I now wish to dance with, I do not know who to choose!" He pushed one hand over his hair, though the smile on his face went against the heavy sigh he let out. "And there shall be so many vying for my attention, I will find myself pulled in all directions."

"Indeed," Lord Dover said, a little dryly. "Now, let us consider *your* situation, Lord Downfield. I have heard so many things recently, I find myself a little irritated!"

Matthew frowned. "I beg your pardon? Whatever can you mean?"

His friends both looked at each other and laughed. "Come now, you cannot think that the *ton* has not noticed the lady's interest in you – her *prolonged* interest! I heard you spoke of it at a gentleman's card game but that you denied any real interest in the lady herself. But it seems that she has continued on in her desire to further her acquaintance with you and, given her standing, one must wonder whether or not you will permit yourself to pursue her."

"Pursue her?" Matthew's head began to buzz with both confusion and a whirlwind of thoughts. He did not know what his friends were speaking about, thinking for a moment that it was to do with Lady Sarah, only for the remark about her high standing to confuse him. She was the daughter of an Earl, yes, but given that he was a Marquess, could it be that his friends thought her of a higher standing than him? Or was it his behavior which made them consider such a thing?

Lord Stephenson nudged Matthew. "There she is. I have been here this evening an hour already and I have heard many a whisper that *you* are the only gentleman she wishes to speak to this evening."

All the more confused, Matthew's gaze fell upon Lady Alice who was, once again, standing with her mother. As he looked to her, the young lady turned her head and caught his eye, only for her face to color and her eyes to dart away.

Matthew's stomach dropped. "You cannot think, gentlemen, that my attention is drawn to Lady Alice, surely?"

"Why would it not be?" Lord Dover asked, as Lord Stephenson nodded fervently. "I understand that when I first came to speak to you about her, you were less than pleased at the notion of showing a genuine interest but think about what you could gain from a connection with the daughter of a Duke! It would give you all that you ever desired!"

A sudden tug of longing seared Matthew's heart and he swallowed tightly, shaking his head as he battled the old familiar urge to push himself forward, to make himself as great – if not greater – than any other gentleman in London in terms of his standing. "I cannot court the lady. I cannot think of matrimony at this present moment. I – I would lose so much."

"What would you lose?" Lord Stephenson challenged, as Matthew began to scowl. "You have no interest in matrimony, I can understand, but there is still ground to be gained from a connection to the lady. And what is matrimony, anyway? It does not mean that you would have to do anything more than you do at present – talk with acquaintances, enjoy society – but you would simply have a young lady on your arm instead!"

Matthew flung out his hands, a fire beginning to build in his stomach. "Enough of this! I want to hear no more. I am not in the least bit interested in the idea, nor in whatever connection it might bring me. Do not speak to me of her again."

The two gentlemen glanced at each other, leaving Matthew feeling a little hot and irritated though he chose to say nothing more.

"I think you are a little foolish not to consider the lady," Lord Dover said, eventually. "You *will* have to go and speak with her and probably dance with her at least once. Otherwise society will certainly think less of you and I know you do not want that."

Matthew gritted his teeth but remained silent, his jaw set tight.

"It cannot be because of that bluestocking of yours," Lord Dover continued, his eyes narrowing as he searched Matthew's face. "That one that you have been spending so much time with? The one playing a foolish game with you – a game which you now appear to be enjoying?"

"I am not enjoying it," Matthew snapped back, his anger curling around him all the more tightly. "Do not speak nonsense, Lord Dover."

"Ah, but you *are* enjoying her company, are you not?" Lord Stephenson asked, his own eyes a little wide as he now turned his attention to Matthew again. "That is what this is about! You do not want to give Lady Alice any attention because you are much too caught up with Lady Sarah."

"A bluestocking. Can you imagine it?"

Seeing the almost disgusted look on Lord Dover's face as he spoke made Matthew's anger turn to a fury which practically enveloped him. He pressed his teeth hard together in order to force himself not to speak, certain that is face was going quite red. How dare they speak of Lady Sarah in such a way?

"I know that you would never attach yourself to a bluestocking," Lord Stephenson said, as Lord Dover shuddered in the most obvious manner. "Can you imagine that? Given all that you have been working on, all that you have been attempting to do in improving your reputation and standing at the very top of society, to then attach yourself to a bluestocking?" He laughed and Matthew curled his hands so tight, his fingernails cut into the soft skin in his palms. "That would be dreadful, would it not? You would be made a mockery of! You would be teased mercilessly for deciding to attach yourself to a bluestocking!"

"I am sure that Downfield is well aware of the consequences of doing so," Lord Dover said, a little dryly. "You mayhap should consider speaking a little less to her, Downfield. The *ton* will soon whisper about it and – "

"You do not know that she is a bluestocking," Matthew interrupted, his tone rather fierce though he ignored how surprise etched itself into each of his friend's expressions. "Hear me now, we will *not* engage ourselves in gossip over this young lady. I will not have it."

The silence which followed this grew so great that it took all of Matthew's strength not to continue speaking, not to demand to know whether they understood him. He looked from Lord Dover to Lord Stephenson and then back again, only for Lord Dover to chuckle, making Matthew blink in surprise.

"Ah, I understand you! You are concerned that she will demand more from you, is that not so? She will add further tasks to her little game and you will be quite stuck!" He tapped one side of his nose and then winked. "I understand. I shall not say a word, I assure you."

Lord Stephenson nodded. "Nor will I," he agreed, as Matthew began to stammer, trying to find the words to explain that this was *not* his main concern but that he simply did not want anything to be whispered about Lady Sarah. "Oh, but look! Lady Alice approaches."

The words died on Matthew's lips as the lady and her mother came purposefully to join the three of them, with the Duchess ignoring those who attempted to speak with her as she passed. The desire in Matthew's heart to go and spend time with Lady Sarah, to ask *her* to dance and to converse for as long as he could with her was set to one side as the familiar urgency to do all that he could to make certain of his fine standing in society began to move to the front of his mind.

"Good evening, Lady Alice, Your Grace." He bowed, fighting inwardly against something that had been a part of him for so long. "How very good to see you this evening." Lifting his chin, he tried to smile but the frown on his face would not remove itself. "I do hope you are enjoying it?"

I will not linger. I will not do all I can to have Lady Alice think well of me, nor have the Duchess think highly of me either. I will excuse myself as soon as is polite and go in search of Lady Sarah instead.

And yet somehow, despite his best attempts, Matthew found himself not only signing Lady Alice's dance card but also offering to take her for a turn around the ballroom, losing his inner battle. Lady Sarah remained at the front of his mind, lingered also in his heart but the old desires, everything that he had fought for so long, finally won out.

Matthew hated himself for it.

Chapter Fifteen

I did not see him last evening.

Sarah sighed to herself as she meandered through the London streets, her acquaintances all around her but her own interests dulled. It had been something of a surprise to receive an invitation from Lady Emilia to walk through town with her and some other young ladies but, of course, Sarah had accepted – though, in truth, her mother had refused to permit her to excuse herself! Sarah had, therefore, found herself at Gunters, taking an ice with young ladies that she was not very well acquainted with, before now meandering to the milliner's. None of the young ladies offered her any sort of conversation and Sarah did not join in any of theirs, for she had no interest in discussing which gentlemen were the most foppish, the grandest or the most handsome. Her thoughts were singled on only one gentleman and he was still very much within her heart.

I think I might very well be in love with him.

The thought was not an unpleasant one and nor did it make Sarah's heart quicken with dread or fright. Instead, she found her lips curving into a smile as she turned her head to look at one set of ribbons and then the next, all without really seeing them. This nonsense with her mysteries and his attempts to answer them had faded slowly into the background, leaving her with very little interest in whether or not he found the answers and, for his part, seeming to have very little urgency in doing so. *That* was what made Sarah's heart glad, for if Lord Downfield was interested in her company rather than in simply answering her questions, then did that not offer her some hope? Hope that her own feelings might be returned?

"I did see that he was dancing with her last evening," she heard someone say, though Sarah quickly pulled her interest away and made to walk to another part of the milliner's. "I do wonder if Lord Downfield will ask to court her soon, for if he does, I am sure that the lady will accept him! She appeared to be quite taken with him!"

Sarah stopped dead, her heart pounding, her smile shattering. Lord Downfield was interested in courting someone else? Another young lady? She had never let that thought enter her mind, had never even imagined that such a thing could be. Squeezing her eyes closed at her own foolishness that she could have possibly assumed that his interest lingered only on her, Sarah dropped her head and let out a slow breath, trying to calm her frantically beating heart.

"I am sure that her father, the Duke of Kettering, would have to make quite certain that Lord Downfield fulfilled all that was required for his daughter's husband," the second lady said, as Sarah's eyes began to burn with unshed tears. "There would be many a conversation, I am sure, and I have heard that the Duke of Kettering can be quite severe."

"Though if Lord Downfield was eager enough in his desire for courtship, I am sure he would not be turned away," said the first, "and given what I saw last evening – his dancing and his conversation – I should say that he *is* so."

Sarah stumbled to the door, wrenching it open and hurrying out into the afternoon sunshine. She knew precisely who it was that the two ladies were speaking of, for Lady Alice had been the young lady that Lord Downfield had gone to in haste, abandoning her entirely in the process. He had apologized, yes, but despite all his kind words to her, what if he had been speaking them only to express his contentment for the friendship between them, rather than anything else? Why had she let her heart be so hasty in its emotions? Why had she never once stopped to consider if she was being overeager?

Sniffing, Sarah pulled out her handkerchief and pressed it to her eyes, only to drop her hand down again as she caught the concerned glances from one or two passers-by. Looking around, her eyes caught sight of the bookshop and, knowing the solace it would bring, Sarah hurried towards it, heedless now to the consequences which would follow, should she be discovered there. All she wanted now was a balm for her soul, a bandage to her aching heart.

Stepping inside, she managed a nod and a brief smile to the proprietor before making her way down the rows of books, hurrying to the very back of the bookshop. Once there, and quite certain that she was entirely alone, Sarah dropped her head, closed her eyes and let the pain and embarrassment rake through her.

Tears came but she did not stop them, pressing her handkerchief to each eye in turn so that no tears would fall to her cheeks. How foolish she had been! How ridiculous to believe that she had been in love with the Marquess of Downfield, only to then see that her affections might not be returned! Ought she not to have made certain of that before permitting her heart to open so deeply towards him? Squeezing her eyes closed, Sarah swallowed a sob, having no desire for the sound of her tears to make its way across the bookshop.

"Lady Sarah?"

With a gasp, Sarah turned, one hand clutching at her heart, her eyes wide as she stared up at the gentleman – only to see the concern in Lord Downfield's eyes.

"I was sure I saw you come in here but I could not find you," he said, coming a little closer to her, his voice low and quiet. "Lady Sarah, whatever is the matter?"

His hand reached out and took hers, his fingers gentle but his gaze never leaving her own.

"I – I... it does not matter." Sarah closed her eyes again, taking in a shuddering breath and wishing desperately that he had not seen her enter here. Why did he have to appear when he would bring her only more pain? "Please, do not be concerned."

"But I am concerned," he said, all the more fervently. "You have rushed in here and hidden yourself away and now I see that you have been crying. Please." His thumb ran across the back of her hand, over and over again in a manner that was both soothing and dreadful at the very same time. She wanted to lean into him, to tell him everything, to beg him to reconsider, to see that *she* was all that he might need but instead, Sarah shook her head.

"It is nothing."

"Why will you not tell me?" Lord Downfield reached out for the second time but, rather than take her hand, let his fingers drift down her cheek until he gently tilted up her chin, encouraging her to look back at him. "I can be trusted, Lady Sarah."

"I know you can be."

"Then tell me what brings such tears to your eyes. Is it because I have not yet given you the answer to your third mystery?" The edges of his mouth tipped upwards. "I do have it, however. I know that the lady discovered a Roman villa. *That* was her remarkable discovery, was it not?"

Sarah managed a small smile in return. "Yes, it was."

"So," Lord Downfield continued, with a lift of his shoulders. "Since I have told you of this, since I have given you my answer, you cannot then be sorrowful over my lack of it. Therefore, it must be something else." His hand fell back to his side rather than cupping her chin and Sarah let out a sigh as he did so, though she turned her head so that he would not hear it. Was this as close as she might ever be to him? As near as she would ever stand? The thought of never again having his hand in hers was so dreadful, Sarah's heart tore and fresh tears came rushing to her eyes.

"You are distressed and my heart is pained for you," Lord Downfield exclaimed, albeit in a quiet manner. "Is there nothing I can do to ease your sorrow?"

"You are already doing so," she whispered, closing her eyes so that the tears there would not come any closer and fall to her cheeks. She sniffed and then opened her eyes, only to start in surprise as she looked up again into Lord Downfield's face, seeing that he had drawn closer to her.

"I think very highly of you, Sarah," he said, quietly. "You have shown me so much about myself and yet you have done it with grace, patience and understanding. I want very much to be able to return that in some way."

Sarah shook her head. "There is no need."

"No?" He offered her a lop-sided smile. "Mayhap you will accept a book from me this time, then? This is the second time I have seen you in the bookshop and I must believe that there is a reason for that. Given your knowledge about certain things and your understanding on other matters, might I ascertain that you read a great deal?"

Fear pushed aside all of Sarah's other emotions as she swallowed hard. "I – I will not deny it."

"Some might call you a bluestocking," he said, though there was such gentleness in his voice, it did not sound as though he were either mocking or demanding an answer from her. "A most unfortunate term, I think."

Sarah's heart began to thud wildly all over again as she licked her lips, trying to find an answer that would not push him away. She did not know whether to accept that from him or not, afraid that whatever she did, his response would be to turn from her.

But what does it matter? If he is going to court Lady Alice then it does not matter to him what I am.

She took in a deep breath and straightened her shoulders, aware of how his thumb still ran over her hand. "Yes, I would be called such a thing, Lord Downfield," she said, with as much firmness as she dared. "But, if we are friends, if we have a shared respect for each other, then I must beg of you not to speak of that to anyone in society. My mother and father have gone to great lengths to hide such a thing from the *ton* and… " She dropped her head, a wave of sadness overwhelming her. "If it was found that I had spoken to any gentleman in all of London about my learning and my reading, if it was made known by my own lips that I am a bluestocking, then my father would return me to his estate and force a match upon me."

A long and pronounced silence followed this and though Sarah tried thrice to lift her gaze to his, she could not, so great was her fear over what he would say. She dared not look at his expression, did not want to see what was in his eyes for fear it would be censure. Her whole body trembled, only for Lord Downfield to step forward and, much to Sarah's astonishment, pull her into his arms.

"I can see that this has brought you a great deal of pain," he murmured, as his arms went around her waist, her head so close to his shoulder that Sarah could not help but rest her head upon it. "I am sorry for it."

The wave of sadness broke over Sarah all over again and tears began to fall despite her attempts to hold them back. She did not know what she was crying for, whether it was because of the shame her parents had over her bluestocking ways, or over how wonderful this moment was

– and how she feared it might never be repeated again.

"The reason I ran from the bookshop before, the reason that I cannot have even a single book in my possession, is because my father has stated quite clearly that if I am found either standing in here or reading a book I have purchased, then I will be married to a gentleman he is acquainted with – a gentleman with a dark disposition who is much too old to be a suitable husband for me," she told him, the words beginning to fall from her lips as though they had been waiting there for many a day, desperate to be spoken. "I could not bear the thought of that but the absence of reading in my life has been difficult indeed."

"You should not have to endure such a thing," Lord Downfield told her, stepping back and letting his hands fall to his sides, leaving Sarah feeling a little cold now, her heart pained that his close embrace had come to an end. "I am sorry for that."

She tried to smile but failed miserably. "It is quite all right. My parents seek to find me a match and have stated that no gentleman wishes to have a bluestocking for a bride." Her heart ripped all over again as Lord Downfield frowned and looked away. "You must hope that Lady Alice has not done a great deal of reading."

The moment those words left her mouth, Sarah flushed hot, horrified with her own rushed reply. The pain in her heart had brought those words to her and she had let them fall without even thinking. Taking a step back from him, she bobbed a curtsy, her face hot, her mind screaming at her to take her leave.

"Forgive me. I ought not to pry. Do excuse me, Lord Downfield."

"Wait."

His hand reached out and caught hers, pulling her back

gently. Sarah swallowed her tears as she tried to gaze into his eyes but found the intensity there far too great to manage. Instead, she contented herself by looking somewhere near his left shoulder, her heart clamoring still.

"You think that Lady Alice... " Lord Downfield let out a hiss of breath, released her arm and then shoved his hand through his hair, his fingers raking through it. "Of course you do, for I have given you that impression."

"I – I do not have anything to say on that matter," Sarah stammered, a little confused as to why he appeared so upset. "Forgive me, I should not have said a word about the lady. It is your own choice and – "

"I have no interest in Lady Alice. None whatsoever."

Sarah blinked, her eyes rounding in surprise.

"It is my own foolish self," Lord Downfield grated, throwing up his hands as he stepped away from her and then turned to come directly back towards her. "For years, I have been determined to make myself the most notable, the most talked about, the most excellent of gentlemen in all of London. I fought hard to keep my reputation excellent but I reveled in the attentions of others, though I have never had any intention of pursuing any of the young ladies who offered me their smiles." He scowled and Sarah looked away, not quite certain how she was to respond to such a thing.

"Lady Alice offered me more of the same," he continued, a little darkly. "She did not know it, of course, but her conversation, her interest in me was all that I have been seeking for the last few Seasons, for it elevates me to a new position in society; one where I am favoured by the Duke and Duchess. Yet – and I am ashamed to say it – my interest in Lady Alice was only in what her connection with me might offer. Last evening, at the ball, I was informed that Lady Alice was hopeful not only of speaking with me but dancing with me also, and I fought hard against all that was familiar to me. But I lost that battle and, in doing so, caused you sorrow."

"You did not," Sarah answered quickly, trying to brush away the question.

"Yes, I did," Lord Downfield murmured, his voice growing softer now as he came closer to her – closer than he had ever been before. His head lowered and he looked deeply into her eyes, his breath brushing lightly across her cheek. "I know that I did."

Sarah could not breathe, nor could she move. All she could do was look up into the Marquess' face, everything else falling away. Her worries about her parents finding her in the bookshop, the niggling worry about confessing that she was a bluestocking... all of it faded to nothing. All that mattered in this one moment was Lord Downfield and how close he stood to her.

"Sarah," Lord Downfield breathed, his fingers tentative as they skated lightly across her cheek, then down the column of her neck to her shoulder. It was as though, in saying her name, he was asking her a question, a question that she was suddenly desperate to answer.

"I do not hold anything against you, Lord Downfield, if that is what concerns you," she said, softly. "I can assure you that there is nothing that has, as yet, pushed me away from you. In fact, the only desire in my heart at present is to... " She closed her eyes and trembled, knowing the weight these next few words carried. "The only desire in my heart is to draw closer to you."

Lord Downfield snatched in a breath and Sarah opened her eyes, suddenly afraid that she had spoken too boldly, that this nearness of him to her meant something else entirely – and then, his mouth was on hers.

The worry, the uncertainty and the confusion all faded

as she leaned into his kiss, her hands going up to his shoulders and then around his neck, seemingly of their own accord. One of his arms went around her waist but the other made its way to the nape of her neck, his fingers edging up into her hair. A light tingling spread all through her and she softened all the more against him, feeling herself a little weak at the sensations which coursed through her.

And then, the bell above the bookshop door clanged, telling them that someone else had stepped into the bookshop and the moment was gone. Lord Downfield lifted his head, sighed gently and then pulled back from her, letting her disentangle herself from his arms.

"I do not want to apologise for that, Lady Sarah, but I certainly shall not do such a thing again, not without making my intentions clear." Lord Downfield looked down into her eyes but then stepped back, bowing his head. "Forgive me. I should – I must… " His expression grew confused as he frowned, then rubbed one hand over his eyes. "Forgive me," he said again. "I shall take my leave of you now and spend some time considering what now must be done. I was not expecting for such an intimacy to take place between us."

"Nor was I," Sarah answered, her voice thready and a little weak as she fought to understand what he was doing in rushing away from her in such a hasty fashion. "But that does not mean that you must hurry away from me now, Lord Downfield. Surely we can continue to speak, to talk about our feelings and what we have just shared." Stepping closer to him again, she put one hand on his arm, gazing up into his eyes. "My heart has been yearning for a closeness with you for some time, my desire for your company growing ever stronger. In truth, Lord Downfield, I believe that my affections for you are increasing steadily and I do not want to be parted from you." She spoke with both honesty and a little desperation, seeing the frown on his face and how his eyes darted away from hers as though he did not want any longer to be as close to her as he had been.

"I did not mean to kiss you," he said, quietly. "I *must* go and think about all of this now. Forgive me for stepping away from you so quickly, Lady Sarah. I swear to you that I shall not be too long in my considerations."

Without another word, without so much as another glance towards her, Lord Downfield turned and made his way from her side with seeming haste. Sarah swallowed hard, the tears which had been in her eyes only a few moments ago now returning with an even greater strength. She had felt herself overwhelmed with happiness to be kissed by Lord Downfield, had practically melted into his arms and now he had stepped away from her, telling her that he needed to think, needed to consider all that he felt and had shared with her? That did not bring her any joy, leaving her – instead – with a deep emptiness and sorrow instead of the remarkable delight she had felt before when she had been caught up in his arms. Closing her eyes, Sarah pulled out her handkerchief and, for what was the second time in only a short space of time, wiped away her heavy tears.

Chapter Sixteen

"Another."

Matthew rubbed at his eyes, feeling them gritty. For the last three days, he had only been either in his townhouse or here at Whites, sitting and contemplating what had happened, what he was to do and what would follow thereafter. He did not know how many hours he had been sitting here in Whites for this evening and yet, despite the prolonged length of time, Matthew could not make sense of all that he was feeling for Lady Sarah. He had learned so much about her, had realized just how deep his feelings for her were and when she had not stepped back from his nearness, when she had drawn closer to him and when he had heard her speak with both happiness and anticipation about a closeness growing between them, he had abandoned all sense and had kissed her.

It had been the most wonderful moment of his life.

When the bell had clanged, however, it had broken through the two of them, leaving him to step back from her as he realized all that had taken place... and the significance of what he had done also. In kissing her, he had not only given way to his feelings but he had also practically declared himself to the lady! It was not a small thing to have done so for he was not a rogue, he was not a rake inclined towards taking liberties! That kiss held a great deal of significance and, in seeing that, Matthew found himself quite terrified.

"What am I to do?" Muttering into his glass, Matthew winced as the memory of what he had done and all that he had felt washed over him again.

The sensations which had flooded him as he had kissed her, the way his emotions had run wildly through him and the joy which rang around his heart had all been wonderful, but what he had been left with, as he lifted his head, was the realization that, should he pursue Lady Sarah, should he pursue a connection with her, then he would find himself connected to a bluestocking – and while he himself had no concern in that regard – what did it matter to him if a lady was well read or not? – understanding that the *ton* would not see it in the same light was troubling.

"Yet again, I am fighting myself," he muttered, taking the glass of brandy from the footman's tray before taking a long sip. Why could he not rid himself of this? Why would it not leave him? It was dogged in its attempts to overwhelm him, to remind him of all that would be said of him, should he tie himself to Lady Sarah. Not only would there be remarks about *her* but there would also be many a remark made about him and his connection. There might be teasing, there would certainly be mockery and his reputation, his precious reputation, would be knocked back. Was that what he wanted?

"You look either pensive or a little in your cups."

Matthew scowled as Lord Rutherford came to sit with him. "I am in no mood for your lectures, Rutherford. Nor do I want to hear just how happy and contented you are, for that will bring me no joy. Your connection to Lady Catherine appears to be very strong and the *ton* are, no doubt, happy for you but I cannot find the same contentment."

Lord Rutherford said nothing, though his eyebrows did lift just a little.

"Though that is not to say that I am not glad for you," Matthew added, having no desire for his friend to think ill of him. "Forgive me for my dull mood, Rutherford. I have something I am contemplating and – "

"And you cannot decide whether or not you will court

Lady Sarah?" Lord Rutherford interjected, grinning as Matthew scowled at him. "Yes, my friend, I am well aware of your struggle, even though you have not spoken a word of it to me."

"How can you be aware of it?" Matthew asked, his brow furrowing. "You and I have not spoken of the lady at all."

"Because you have been entirely absent from society for three days now and that can only mean one thing – that your affections are engaged and you know not what to do about them." Lord Rutherford chuckled. "Besides that, I have seen your interest in the lady grow and your consideration of her with it, though I have been concerned that your connection to Lady Alice might affect your heart."

"There *is* no connection between Lady Alice and myself!" Matthew cried, suddenly agitated. "I do not want anyone to think that I am eager to court Lady Alice for that would mean that my interest lay with her and it… well, it does not."

"It lies with Lady Sarah."

Matthew groaned aloud, closing his eyes and throwing his head back to the back of his chair. "Please, Rutherford. Either tell me what I should do or go away."

Lord Rutherford chuckled quietly. "I would be glad to, except for the fact that you have not told me anything specific about what concerns you."

Matthew hesitated, wondering if he ought to tell his friend about the fact that he had not only caught the lady up in his arms but had kissed her also. Sensing that his friend would work that out whether he told him or not, Matthew shrugged. "My feelings for Lady Sarah have reached a particular… height."

"Oh." Lord Rutherford's eyebrows lifted a little higher.

"I presume, then, that she is... how shall I say this? She is *aware* of your feelings?"

"If you are asking me if I kissed her, then the answer is yes." Matthew groaned and ran one hand over his eyes, shutting them tightly for a moment. "I did not mean to. That is, I did not go in to speak with her with the intention of doing so."

Lord Rutherford nodded. "I know you well enough to believe that to be true. You need not have any concern there."

"I thank you."

His friend shrugged. "So what is it that troubles you, then? The lady is clearly as interested in your company and your connection as you, so I cannot see why you are sitting here, confused and perturbed. There should be joy in your heart at this, should there not be?"

Matthew shook his head, sighed and then took another sip from his glass so that he could have a few extra moments by which to consider his answer. "There mayhap should be, yes," he admitted, as Lord Rutherford listened carefully. "But I walked away from her, Rutherford. I left her without promise nor hope." He winced at the shock which quickly wrote itself across his friend's expression. "I did not mean to be in the least bit cruel but my emotions were so weighty and the realization of what that could now mean began to race through my mind with such speed, I found myself quite caught up with... well, I do know precisely what emotion it was but my desire was to step away and to let myself think clearly about all that had just taken place."

Lord Rutherford sniffed. "You are afraid."

"I – " Matthew opened his mouth and then grimaced, realizing that his friend was speaking the truth.

"You are afraid of your own emotions for, no doubt,

you have never experienced such a connection as this before and now, given that the future is quite clear not only to me but to you also, you are refusing to face that truth and so, instead, have stepped away from it all."

Matthew swallowed hard, hating the truth which was being offered to him. "It is not that."

"Yes it is."

"It is not!" he exclaimed, trying to explain to his friend that it was not all as he believed. "She is a bluestocking."

Lord Rutherford blinked, then shrugged. "So? What does that matter?" When Matthew did not answer, Lord Rutherford's eyes rounded as understanding washed over him, only for him to snort in evident derision before looking away. "My dear friend, I am *quite* right," he said, making Matthew's scowl reappear with great swiftness. "It *is* because of fear that you are sitting here rather than doing as you truly wish to do deep down in your heart, which is to go and court Lady Sarah. You fear that in being connected to her, your reputation will somehow suffer. This precious reputation of yours, the one you have held in higher esteem than any living soul, might now be tainted, all because the lady you have come to care for has a great deal of knowledge and understanding." He snorted, then rolled his eyes. "I thought that you had learned that the pride within you and the arrogance which held you in its sway were both things to be set aside, no? I thought that your connection with Lady Sarah had taught you something and that you, in turn, were moving away from it. Is that not so now? You have decided to cling to who you were, rather than move forward into the gentleman you were becoming, the one who was doing his level best to set all that aside? I know that you were having difficulties in your connection with Lady Alice and that you were fighting between the desire to have her close in order to elevate you all the more in society and turning, instead, to Lady Sarah, but am I to believe now that you have chosen the former instead of the latter?"

"I – I have not chosen anything," Matthew stammered, a little overwhelmed by Lord Rutherford's tirade. "Come now, you cannot think me as much of a fool as that? I will not step away from the lady without good reason."

"And the good reason would be your reputation?"

Matthew paused, then shook his head. "No, that is not what I meant."

"Then what did you mean?"

There was nothing for Matthew to say. The truth was quite clear, both to his friend and to himself and, deep in his heart, Matthew was ashamed of it. He cared deeply for Lady Sarah, he knew that, more deeply than he had ever cared for anyone and yet the thing that was pushing him back from her, the one thing that held him away from her was the knowledge that the *ton* would soon find out that she was a bluestocking – for he would not force her to hide it, as her parents had done – and he would have the whispers and the gossip and the rumors all rushing around him. The *ton* would laugh that he was engaged or wed to a bluestocking, mocking him for requiring such a thing in a wife and, of course, looking down upon Lady Sarah herself, though Matthew doubted that the lady herself would give that even a single moment of thought.

"You need to set aside this reputation of yours for the sake of love." Lord Rutherford took in a deep breath and then sat forward in his chair, his gaze steady. "You care for Lady Sarah, no doubt you probably love her though you will not admit it to me, and that is what is most important. To set that aside, to leave as though she means very little to you will only cause you pain. Tell me, my friend, does it concern you in any way that she is a learned young lady? That she is a bluestocking?"

Matthew shook his head. "No, of course not."

"Then why should you care if the *ton* think differently? Why should you take even the smallest notice of it? I know that you have often given in to the fear of what society thinks of you but does it not matter to you all the more what Lady Sarah's opinion is of you?" Lord Rutherford tipped his head just a little. "You have a young lady who cares for you, my friend. Do you know how fortunate you are in that regard? Do you not understand what a gift you have been given?"

A nudge of shame pushed into Matthew's heart. "I – I might not have seen it in such a light before."

"Then see it now," Lord Rutherford stated, firmly. "You have a beautiful, intelligent, genteel young lady who returns your affections and who, might I add, has endured a great deal of hurt at your behaviour towards her – which includes your foolishness in walking away from her just after you shared a kiss for, no doubt, she was left feeling empty and foolish."

Matthew dropped his head.

"I say this not to heap shame on you but to make you understand what you have by way of Lady Sarah's heart. It is an incredible blessing, a joy which so few have to claim. You have been fighting against your desires to return to the *ton* as you were before, doing all you could to make your name known and to lift it higher than almost everyone else in society. The only way to win, Downfield, the only way to gain that security is to make certain that you do the opposite of whatever your mind is telling you to do."

Matthew lifted his head. "What do you mean?"

"It tells you to run from Lady Sarah, to set your back to her so that the *ton* will not know that you have connected yourself to a bluestocking. Your heart tells you that you must run to her, that you must offer her your heart, your hand, your entire life, if you can, given all that she has become to you. What you *must* do, if you are to be free of this, is to do what your heart says rather than your mind. Do the opposite of what your mind tells you and, instead, turn to your heart. Listen to that rather than to your thoughts. I know it is not the thing that you usually do but I promise you that, should you do so, you will find yourself happier – though the thought might be a little terrifying, I am sure."

"Mayhap a little," Matthew muttered, shoving one hand through his hair and letting out a long, slow breath. Lord Rutherford was quite right, he knew, and yet it was just as he had said: the thought of doing that very thing, of turning to Lady Sarah and offering her his heart, knowing what would follow, was a somewhat terrifying one.

"You will be happier for it, I know," his friend told him, firmly. "Now that I have Lady Catherine by my side, now that I know we are to become engaged and wed – and yes, you need not look at me like that for it is not something I have discussed with you as yet, though I have discussed it with the lady – I find that nothing else in my life is of any concern. I do not care what the *ton* thinks, nor do I find myself desiring to be in society's company. All that I want is Lady Cahterine, I want to be with her and with her alone. My mind has nothing but thoughts of her, of her happiness and joy rather than worrying about what anyone else should say of either myself or my connection to the lady."

"But Lady Catherine is not a bluestocking."

"Even if she were, would it make any difference?" Lord Rutherford asked, his eyes twinkling. "I can assure you, it would not. I was drawn to her beauty, her strength and her tenacity and that has not changed. I have no doubt that there will be some in the *ton* who think that a lady ought not to speak as firmly nor as bluntly as she does, some who will comment on her behaviour and say that it is inappropriate but I can assure you that there is nothing in that which concerns me. In fact, I could not care any less about it! He smiled. "So it will be with Lady Sarah, so long as you are willing to make that decision and turn away from your fear of what the *ton* will say of it all. They will not bring you happiness no matter what you do, I can assure you. But Lady Sarah certainly shall do and I believe that you know that already."

Matthew threw back the rest of his brandy rather than respond to his friend. He had no doubt that Lord Rutherford was correct in what he stated but he himself was growing a little weary of the conversation, finding his spirits sinking as he realized, yet again, how foolishly he had behaved when it had come to Lady Sarah. At the time of their kiss, he had known precisely what it was he had wanted, eager to have more of her company, of her closeness and of her kisses – and that meant courtship, if not engagement and matrimony.

And yet, his own ridiculous concerns over high standing and the like had driven him away from her arms rather than encouraging him to linger.

How idiotic he had been.

"I would rather not speak of this any longer," he muttered, gesturing to the footman for another. "I can see that you are correct in everything you have said and, therefore, given my present mortification and shame, I should like to bring an end to the conversation."

Lord Rutherford looked back steadily. "I do not mean to place any sort of shame upon you."

"I bring it upon myself," Matthew answered, darkly. "I thank you for your boldness in speaking to me as you do,

Lord Rutherford. We are friends indeed, are we not?"

"We are." Lord Rutherford got up and, after a moment, shook Matthew's hand. "I do hope that I will soon be able to offer you my congratulations?"

Matthew allowed a smile to edge up the corner of his mouth. "You have convinced me to do what my heart wants rather than listen to my thoughts, yes," he said, feeling a knot tie itself in his stomach even as he said those words. "Thank you, my friend. I hope that very soon, I will be free of all the fear that has held me for so long – and that instead, I will hold Lady Sarah close to me."

Chapter Seventeen

Sarah's hands twisted in front of her as she walked into the ballroom, her eyes searching for the one face, the one person she was desperate to see. It had been three days since he had kissed her in the bookshop, three days since he had hurried away thereafter and three days since she had been left wondering how long it would be before he would reach out to her again. Her fears had mounted, leaving her filled with a deep sense of dread that would not leave her. What if he was to tell her that there could be no deepening of their connection? What if that kiss had, in some way, told him that they were not meant to be, despite how much she herself thought it? Her heart would be quite broken if he turned away from her entirely but, given the silence from him, given that there had been no notes, no coming to take tea and, indeed, his absence from social events, Sarah's hopes were slowly beginning to crack.

"You do look rather pale this evening." Lady Harcastle turned to face Sarah, her expression one of concern. "Pinch your cheeks before we go any further, so that no gentleman sees you in such a state."

Sarah obeyed, looking away as she did so. "Mama, there is something… " She trailed off as her mother looked away, clearly paying no attention to anything that Sarah was saying. She closed her eyes briefly, her face hot now that she had done as her mother had asked. Quite what she had been about to say, Sarah was not certain but the desire to unburden herself, even a little, was strong. Lady Catherine had been quite taken up with Lord Rutherford, and Sarah had heard words about engagement and the like, so she could well understand her friend's excitement. That being said, she had found it difficult that Lady Catherine had not asked about Lord Downfield and as such, Sarah had spent the last three days feeling rather lonely.

"There you are!" Lady Catherine, the very person that Sarah had been thinking about, hurried forward and, after greeting Lady Harcastle, beamed at Sarah. "I have been looking all over for you."

"Have you?" Sarah tried to smile, her own spirits nowhere near the heights of Lady Catherine's. "I have only just arrived. Is there a reason that you were looking for me with such enthusiasm?"

"Only because I think that, this evening, Lord Rutherford intends to make his proposal!" Lady Catherine squealed, pulling Sarah a little closer as they walked, arm in arm, around the ballroom as they usually did. "He has sought permission from my father and been granted it!"

"How wonderful!" Sarah's heart tore though she forced a smile, trying to set aside her own unhappiness. "I assume you will accept?"

Lady Catherine laughed heartily. "Of course I shall!" She smiled and then looked to Sarah, though her smile faltered a little. "Might I ask if there is something troubling you, my dear friend? You seem a little pale this evening."

Sarah swallowed hard, trying to keep her emotions under control. "I – I have had some difficulty of late, as regarded Lord Downfield."

"Oh." Lady Catherine stopped walking and then pulled her arm from Sarah's. "And I have been far too caught up with my own affairs to notice. Tell me, my dear. Tell me all."

It was all that Sarah needed. The tide of emotion broke over her and, with a quavering voice and eyes that were already damp with unshed tears, she told Lady Catherine everything. Her friend led her to a quiet corner where Sarah continued to speak, keeping her voice as low as she could but holding nothing back.

At the end, she felt herself worn out, as though she had given all of her strength simply to speaking. With a heavy heart, Sarah closed her eyes and dropped her head. "And now, I have been waiting for him for some three days. He said he has much to think about but what is there to consider? Either we are to form a connection or we are not!"

"Indeed, but you know that Lord Downfield is a complicated gentleman, do you not? You know of his pride and his arrogance and how great a hold they had on his character." Lady Catherine tilted her head and smiled sympathetically. "This is how it has all come about, is it not? You thought that playing these little mysteries with Lord Downfield might encourage him not only to see the difference between Tom Jones and himself– initially, at least – but also to thereafter, alter his character somewhat. Now that it has, now that he has begun to change, can you not see that it will take time for him to improve entirely?"

"You mean that he must battle all that he knows? All that he has been and now no longer wants to be?"

Lady Catherine nodded. "And though I am loathe to say this, you must prepare yourself for the chance that he might not change into the gentleman that you desperately wish him to be. There is a chance that he will turn his back on all he feels for the sake of his reputation."

Sarah's gut twisted. "Because I am a bluestocking, because he knows of it and that the *ton* will hear of it also."

Lady Catherine reached out and took Sarah's hand in hers. "Yes," she said, simply. "It brings me no joy to say this, I can assure you. It is only said out of concern."

Closing her eyes against the swell of fresh tears, Sarah nodded slowly as her heart, which had held so little hope already, finally lost the last few trickles of it. The silence from Lord Downfield, the absence of his presence from society told her that all was not well. She would be rejected, their connection would be severed and he would return to who he had once been, chasing the highest elevation for himself within society.

"Lady Sarah?"

At a tap on her shoulder, Sarah turned around, only to see a young lady standing there, a slight lift to her chin and a flicker of dislike in her eyes. "Yes?"

"I hear that you are acquainted with Lord Downfield."

"Yes, I am," Sarah replied, looking to Lady Catherine who, for some reason, had gone very still indeed. "Though I do not think that we are acquainted."

The young lady sniffed. "I do not think that we need to be. What I must say to you can be spoken and then our connection can end." Her lips curved into a smile but it was not one that brought Sarah any warmth. Indeed, there was a coldness there which she shuddered to see, worrying as to what it was that this young lady was going to say.

"I do not understand," she told her, as firmly as she could. "If we are not acquainted, then why must you speak with me?"

"It is about Lord Downfield."

Sarah blinked rapidly, trying to hide her surprise. "What is it you wish to say to me about him? Surely anything you have to speak about, you ought to say to him directly?"

The young lady's lips curved all the more but there was ice in her gaze. "Not when it comes to your connection with him, Lady Sarah," she said, her voice more like a hiss than anything else. "You will cease your connection with him at once. It will come to an end. You will tell him that you have no interest in even being acquainted with him any longer and you will treat him as though you have never seen him before in your life."

Rather astonished at this, a ball of harsh laughter stuck in Sarah's throat, though she managed to pull it back. "I hardly think that you have any right to demand such things of me," she said, as Lady Catherine took a step closer in what Sarah saw as a show of solidarity. "There is no reason for me to treat Lord Downfield with such disregard and I can assure you that I have no intention of doing so."

"No?" The lady's smile fell, crashing to the floor. "I am afraid, Lady Sarah, that if you do not do as I have asked, then I will have no choice but to tell society that you are nothing more than a bluestocking. I will tell all of society that you delve into matters that no young lady ought to know about, that you pry and snoop into all manner of affairs. The *ton* will know of it all and then what will become of you?"

The shock of her words ricocheted around Sarah's heart, causing her to stumble back. She stared at the young lady, confused and horrified at what had been said, of the threats which had been laid at her door.

"Lady Alice, this is entirely unfair," she heard Lady Catherine say, her voice seeming to come from very far away. "Why ever should you demand Lady Sarah to do such a thing? That is not how we ought to treat one another, it is – "

"I do not care to hear whether or not you approve of what I am doing," Lady Alice interjected, swiping her hand through the air. "All I wish to do is to hear that Lady Sarah agrees with me."

"I – I do not agree with you," Sarah breathed, her whole body shuddering as she spoke. "I do not think it right for you to speak to me in this manner and I certainly will not agree to step away from Lord Downfield. He and I are good friends and – "

"And do you think that you will continue to be so once the *ton* knows you are a bluestocking?" Lady Alice's lip curled. "Do you believe that he will stand by your side and insist that yes, you *are* his dear acquaintance and that he cares nothing for the fact that you are what you are?"

Recalling the quick way that Lord Downfield had stepped back from her once they had shared a kiss, doubt began to swirl through Sarah's mind but she did not let her stance falter. The shock of Lady Alice's demands had begun to lessen and now, Sarah lifted up her chin a little more, refusing to let the lady win this battle. Yes, she had a great and dreadful fear that Lady Alice would tell everyone about her bluestocking ways and what would become of that, but neither was she willing to buckle under the weight that Lady Alice was placing upon her! To agree to this would be to agree to remove herself from Lord Downfield's company for good and the thought of that was much too painful even to consider for long.

"It would only to be Lady Alice's word," Lady Catherine whispered, turning her head so that Lady Alice could not see her speak. "I could defend you. There are others who would consider it only gossip and if needs be, I would be more than willing to support you as you defend yourself to your parents in the hope of convincing them not to return you to your father's estate."

Sarah looked back at her friend, her stomach twisting as she fought fear. "It would be viewed as gossip, would it not?"

Lady Catherine nodded. "She has no proof of what she will say."

Taking in a deep breath, Sarah set her shoulders and gave her friend a nod. "I must also trust Lord Downfield, that he would not turn away from me even if society thought ill of me."

"Indeed."

Still afraid of what consequences her answer would bring, Sarah turned her attention back to Lady Alice, aware that she still shook a little from both dread and shock. "I trust Lord Downfield, that he would not turn from me. Your words about me being a bluestocking would be seen as only gossip. Therefore, I am afraid that I cannot do as you have asked."

"I think you have your answer, Lady Alice," Lady Catherine said, her smile encouraging Sarah but clearly angering Lady Alice, who immediately began to scowl. "I do not think we need to continue this conversation any longer, do you?"

Sarah continued to tremble but kept her expression as calm as she could and her gaze steady. She was not about to be coerced into doing anything though what her future might now hold was terrifying indeed. If Lady Alice did as she had threatened, then Sarah might find herself dragged back to her father's estate and wed to some dreadful gentleman in his dotage! But yet she had to trust that, even with those consequences looming heavily, she still had hope and that was enough to fight for.

"Very well." Lady Alice's scowl grew all the darker as she came a little closer, her eyes narrowing. "And what will you say if I tell you that, should you refuse to turn from Lord Downfield, should you refuse to move away from him as I have asked, then I will spread rumours about *him*, rumours which will quite ruin his reputation."

A darkness draped itself around Sarah's shoulders.

"No doubt you will tell me that many a rumour has been said about many a gentleman and that those rumours simply swirl through society for a time before fading away. And yet, I shall then go on to remind you that I am the daughter of a Duke and that my words are more likely to be both listened to and believed."

"Why would you do such a thing?" Lady Catherine asked, as Sarah's heart thudded dully in her chest. "Why would you whisper gossip about a gentleman who has done you no wrong?"

"Oh, but he has! I have seen that his interest is more in Lady Sarah than in my own company, I have seen that he does not eagerly choose my company despite what the *ton* might say."

"Then why do you demand that I stay away from him?" Sarah asked, her voice a good deal quieter than before. "Why would you expect this from me?"

"Because," Lady Alice answered, shrugging her shoulders, "I have decided that he is the gentleman I wish to court me and therefore, I shall have what I desire. You are in my way, Lady Sarah, and if you do not do as I ask then I shall ruin your reputation."

"But you would ruin his also?"

Lady Alice shrugged. "If I cannot have him pursue me, then I shall not permit him to pursue anyone either. He will be ruined, his reputation will be covered in dirt and that shall bring me a great deal of contentment. Thereafter, I shall turn my attention again to the *ton* and see which gentleman next catches my eye. Though, of course, I do not have to do anything of the sort to him, Lady Sarah. That choice is yours."

Lady Catherine grasped Sarah's wrist as though she knew what was on the tip of Sarah's tongue and wanted to prevent it but Sarah spoke before she could do so.

"You believe that he will pursue you once I pull myself back from him?" she asked, her voice hoarse now. "That is your thinking?"

Lady Alice nodded. "It is."

"And what if he does not?"

A small, cruel smile touched the edge of Lady Alice's lips. "Then I shall inform him that he must."

Seeing that the lady fully expected to gain what she pleased in whatever way she wished, Sarah dropped her head and closed her eyes. She did not want to step away from him, did not want to end their connection but now, it seemed, she was going to be forced away from him regardless of her own desires.

"You do not have to do this," Lady Catherine whispered, as tears began to burn behind Sarah's eyes. "You do not have to do as she asks."

"I must," Sarah answered, softly. "I must, for I have to protect Lord Downfield. I cannot permit him to be so injured."

Lady Catherine shook her head but Sarah opened her eyes and looked straight at her friend. "My dear friend, if there is something else that you can suggest, then please, tell me of it now." When Lady Catherine shook her head and pressed her lips flat together, Sarah let out a slow breath and then shrugged her shoulders. There was nothing for her to do but to agree with Lady Alice's demands, knowing that she would be stepping away from Lord Downfield forever. "Very well, Lady Alice," she finished, hopelessly. "I will inform Lord Downfield of my decision to step back from him very soon."

"This evening. Oh, and you are not to give him any explanation as to why this is happening, else the consequences I have spoken of will fall upon him – and you – regardless."

Sarah closed her eyes. "Please, I – "

"This evening, Lady Sarah," Lady Alice interrupted, firmly. "Good evening to you both."

She walked away and Sarah wanted to cry out, wanted

to do something, to say anything that would stop this situation from taking place, something that would bring an end to all of Lady Alice's plans but, in the end, the only thing that remained was her agreement.

"You are truly going to tell Lord Downfield that you can no longer be in company with him?"

Nodding, Sarah closed her eyes, feeling dampness on her cheeks.

"And what if he asks you why?"

Shaking her head, Sarah took the handkerchief that Lady Catherine pressed into her hand. "I do not know what I shall say. Mayhap I will simply inform him of it and walk away even though my heart will break as I do so."

"Can you really turn your back on such a strong affection?" Lady Catherine asked, softly. "Can you not go to him and explain all that has happened, even with all that Lady Alice has threatened?"

"He has not come back to my company ever since we shared that kiss," Sarah answered, her heart ripping into pieces. "There might not have been any hope for me anyway."

"Do not say that!" Lady Catherine exclaimed. "It may be that he was simply overwhelmed with the emotion of it all and, now that he has considered it all, looks instead to come to speak with you about a happy future! Are you going to throw that chance away by refusing to say a single word?"

"I dare not be truthful," Sarah whispered, her head still hanging low as all hope fled from her. "If anything should happen to him, if anything should come from the risk I would take in speaking honestly to him, then I would never forgive myself. I care about him too much to ever risk that."

Lady Catherine put a hand to Sarah's arm. "You love him?"

Shaking her head, Sarah lifted her gaze to her friend's face. "I do not know. It is a foolishness to love someone who has shown no determination to pull himself close to me after we shared such an intimacy but I will admit that my heart is determined to do such a thing regardless. Whether that is love, I cannot say for certain, but all I know is that, when I speak to Lord Downfield about this, it will shatter into a million pieces and, I am sure, will never be able to be restored again."

Chapter Eighteen

"My friend." Lord Rutherford clapped a hand on Matthew's shoulder, then frowned as Matthew continued to twist his head this way and that, in search of someone. "Might I ask what it is you are doing at present? Your imitation of an owl is to be commended but –"

"I seek Lady Sarah." Matthew shot his friend a wry look, though Lord Rutherford only grinned. "I have come to a determination and now must go in search of her."

"You intend to speak of your future with her this evening?"

Matthew threw him another wry look. "Mostly, Lord Rutherford, I intend to apologise. That is all that is required of me at present, I think. I will go to her and beg her to forgive my foolishness in walking away from her as I did. I will express my sorrow for causing her yet more pain and then express my astonishment that she should ever be willing to spend yet more time in my company!"

Lord Rutherford nodded. "And if she tells you that she forgives you and that yes, her affections are still engaged, then what are your intentions?"

Matthew smiled, his heart leaping at the thought. "I hope to ask her to court me, in the full awareness that she is a bluestocking and that the *ton*, at some point, will know of it. In addition, I also intend to go to her father and state that I am aware of how learned she is and how I consider that to be an admirable and respectable quality. I do not want them to think for a moment that I will be turned back from the lady simply because of how much she reads and how much she understands! They have treated that as if it is something to be hidden but I have no intention of doing that myself."

"I see." Lord Rutherford's expression grew thoughtful. "That is an excellent thing, I must say. I am sorry to hear that her parents have not been as encouraging as they ought to have otherwise been but if you are to champion that in her, then I am sure it will mean a great deal to the lady."

"I must hope so," Matthew answered, offering a small smile to his friend. "I should thank you also for all that you have done in pushing me forward in this. You have often attempted to point out the pride in me, I know, and I have been less than willing to listen to you but I am grateful for it now. Lady Sarah forced that realization upon me and in doing so, made me realize how much weight I place upon the *ton* and their view of me. It has taken a long time and, I am sure, a great deal of patience both from Lady Sarah and from yourself, but I am now truly an altered gentleman."

"Good." Lord Rutherford winked. "Then I am not to see you pursuing Lady Alice any longer?"

Matthew laughed, then winced. "I never thought to pursue her," he said, honestly. "It was always for my own, selfish ends though I have turned from that now. I do not ever wish to return to that place again so, therefore, I turn my back on all that held itself tight to me before." He lifted his head. "I am reformed. I am renewed and I declare that I am now devoted to Lady Sarah and her happiness."

Lord Rutherford beamed. "Wonderful! And just in time, I think, for look, the lady approaches now!"

Matthew turned expectantly, his heart suddenly quickening as he looked into Lady Sarah's face, recalling how he had kissed her, how her lips had softened against his and how much his heart had yearned for more. "Lady Sarah." He bowed and then reached for her hand, bowing over it for the second time. "How glad I am to see you this evening." Looking to her friend, he bowed again. "And Lady Catherine,

Lady Sarah's stalwart friend. I am glad to see you here this evening also, and grateful for all that you have ever said to me, for it has forced me into a reconsideration of myself."

Lady Catherine's eyes rounded, though she blinked quickly and then gestured to Lady Sarah. "No doubt most of this was brought about by Lady Sarah however, yes?"

"Yes, of course." Matthew smiled warmly at Lady Sarah, though his brows furrowed when she did not return it, instead looking away. "Though there is much that I need to say to you still, Lady Sarah. A good deal of apology and explanation."

Lady Sarah closed her eyes, dragged in a breath and, opening her eyes again, looked straight at him. "Our connection must come to an end, Lord Downfield."

It was as though he had been punched hard in the stomach, staring at the lady in utter shock. He tried to speak but the only sound out of his mouth was a squeak.

"I am afraid that I cannot explain to you as to why this must be," Lady Sarah continued, though Matthew caught a glint of tears in her eyes. "But it must be done and it must be done this evening. I cannot speak another word to you from this moment onwards."

"Wait." His voice hoarse, Matthew reached out and caught her wrist, his hand wrapping gently around it and Lady Sarah did not struggle, though she turned her head as though she could not bear to look at him. "I know why this is, Sarah. I understand what it is you are doing but it is not as you think!" Desperation rushed over him and he took a step closer, though Lady Sarah began to walk away, half pulling, half guiding him with her. "This is because I walked away from you, that I disappeared without a word and then spent the next three days absent from you," he continued, as she hurried to the back of the ballroom before wrenching her wrist out of his grasp. "Please, Sarah, do not turn from me now! We are so very close to perfect happiness – a happiness which, I know, I have pulled us away from. I should never have done such a foolish thing as to walk away from that moment. I should never have even *thought* about doing that and yet, in my confusion and my fear, I did."

"Fear?" Lady Sarah looked back at him now, tears filling her eyes. "You were afraid?"

"Yes." Matthew's face burned with shame but he kept his gaze steady, choosing to tell her everything clearly. "I was afraid because the old part of myself, the part that I have begun to fight daily, reared its head once more. I thought only about the *ton,* wondering what they would think of me, should I begin to court a bluestocking. I spent three days thinking of my future, wrestling with the feelings of my heart and the old worries which continued to throw themselves up at me. And then I realised just how much of a fool I was being, reminded by my friend Lord Rutherford just what had brought me to this place and then, to my shame, seeing how much pain and sorrow my actions would have brought you." With a sigh, he passed one hand over his eyes and shook his head, his gut twisting as he saw the sadness etched across Lady Sarah's face. "I care for you a great deal, Sarah. My heart holds a great and wonderful affection for you and I care nothing for the fact that you are a bluestocking. In fact, I think it marvelous – an *excellent* thing, and I have an extensive library which I would be delighted to show you one day."

"I... " Lady Sarah squeezed her eyes closed and much to Matthew's dismay, a tear fell to her cheek.

"Here, please." Agony tore at every part of him as he pulled out a handkerchief and offered it to her. "I can see just how much pain I have caused you and I swear to you, should you give me one more chance, then I will never do such a thing again. I have learned all that you have wanted me to learn and, in doing so, I have found myself quite lost in my affections for you. You are the most remarkable, wonderful, incredible, beautiful and delightful lady of my acquaintance, with an abundance of patience, kindness and wisdom within your heart. I have acted with stupidity and selfishness and yet, should you permit me one final chance to draw close to you, I can promise you that I would never do such a thing again."

Lady Sarah shook her head. "I – I cannot."

"Why?" Matthew moved closer to her, heedless to the others present, his eyes searching hers. "You cannot forgive me? Is that it?"

"No, I swear it has nothing to do with that." Lady Sarah closed her eyes again, then dabbed at them with his handkerchief. "I will not step back from anything I have said to you previously, Downfield. I will cling to them all the more tightly, I will declare them to you again, should you wish it. And yet, I must remove myself from your company. I cannot be seen with you again."

A flash came into Matthew's mind. "Is this your fourth and final mystery?" he asked, clinging to the faint hope that this, somehow, might be some sort of drama by which to confuse him. "I know that we have not completed the final one and I must hope that this is what all your tears are for."

Lady Sarah smiled sadly but did not give him the answer he had been looking for. "If only it were."

"Then tell me why you must do this," Matthew begged, his heart beginning to hammer furiously as Lady Sarah shook her head again. "There is some reason that you cannot tell me this, is there not?"

She looked at him, then nodded.

"But you will not tell me what it is?"

"It is not that I will not, but that I cannot." Glancing around her, something like fear crept into her eyes and Matthew frowned heavily. "I must take my leave of you now, Downfield. Please, despite all that you might wish to do, do not pursue me. It is for your best if you do not."

"No." He came closer to her now, barely more than a few inches between them. "I am at my best when I am *close* to you, Sarah. I cannot abandon you now, not when I can tell that there is something severe present, something that is painful for you."

Her eyes closed again as though shutting out the sight of him would give her the courage to do or say what was required. Matthew caught her hand in his, as surreptitiously as he could manage, and caught the small sigh which came from the lady.

"I must go," she said, hoarsely. "Please, Downfield." Her eyes opened, tears spilling from them. "I must go."

Matthew's jaw tightened. "I will count this as your fourth mystery," he told her, releasing her hand and stepping back despite the urge to do precisely the opposite. "If you cannot tell me, then I will discover the truth regardless and, when I do, I will solve the difficulty and, thereafter, return to you. I will not let what might be crumble before our eyes because of some... some difficulty." His eyes searched her face. "If I did so, Lady Sarah, would you return to my arms? Would you be willing to consider me?"

She blinked rapidly, her lips trembling. Taking in a breath, she gave him a small, almost imperceptible nod, and then, without any further words to him, stepped away.

It took all of Matthew's strength not to follow after her. He let his gaze linger on her form as she moved through the crowd until he lost sight of her completely. It was only then that he dropped his gaze, ran one hand over his hair and let out a long, heavy sigh.

Something was very wrong indeed but quite how he was to go about solving this final mystery, he did not know. Turning, Matthew's gaze ran over each face near him, his breathing quick and fast, one hand clenched into a fist as he tried to think clearly, tried to come up with an idea of what he was to do first.

Lady Catherine.

A small, firm smile caught the edge of his mouth and, without a second of hesitation, Matthew strode back into the crowd and went in search of the one lady who might be able to give him some more clarity.

***

"Lady Catherine, there you are."

"I am present also, Downfield," Lord Rutherford said, a little indignantly, but Matthew had no time to answer. Instead, he came a little closer to Lady Catherine and held her gaze, silently praying that she would tell him something. Lady Catherine blinked, then frowned before her mouth tugged to one side, as if she were struggling to know whether she ought to speak.

"You know something about what has taken place, I can see," Matthew murmured, as quietly as he dared. "I care for your friend. I may not have been the most sensible of gentlemen of late – I will admit that I have treated her without the consideration that she is due – but I wish to amend that. Except now, she has no time to give me and when I ask her if it is because of my previous foolishness, she assures me it is not! But neither will she tell me what it is that pulls her from me."

"I can assure you, it is not because of your actions nor your behaviour towards her that she had to move away from you again," Lady Catherine said, though her eyes held a great deal of sadness as she spoke to him. "You can be assured that she does not want this, Lord Downfield. She does not *want* to be apart from you."

"Then why does she step back?"

Lady Catherine closed her eyes and shook her head. "I do not think that I can tell you. It is not my place to do so."

"But you *must*!" Matthew exclaimed, coming closer to her, his fears beginning to rise with such strength, he could not help himself, speaking now with great fervor. "I will be lost without her, Lady Catherine, lost! I have been foolish enough not to give her all of my heart and all of my attentions for a long time, I have been idiotic in giving way to my fears and to my own selfishness. Now, when I finally realise how much of a fool I have been, I do the only thing I can and throw myself upon her mercies in the hope that her affections might still come to me. And though I believe that they do – and knowing how unworthy I am of her considerations – I find myself now utterly distraught that she feels herself forced in some manner to pull herself away from me and from what future happiness we might have had. Please, if you can give me anything, even the smallest morsel, I shall be glad of it for I must find a way to solve this, if I can. I must discover even the smallest bit of truth so I can bring her back to myself, if she still wishes it."

Lady Catherine searched his face for a long time, then she sighed softly and shook her head. "There have been threats made, though I dare not speak of them plainly," she began, offering Matthew a tiny fragment of hope. "As you yourself have seen, there is no real desire within her to step back from what you had begun to share but yet, she feels that she must in order to protect… " Closing her eyes, she trailed off.

"She needs to protect herself," Matthew breathed, his hands curling into tight fists. "Who has threatened her? What has been said?"

Lady Catherine opened her eyes again and looked straight back at him. "No, Lord Downfield," she said, softly. "Lady Sarah does not seek to protect herself. Indeed, when the threats were first made, she rejected them entirely, stating aloud that she did not care one iota for what might happen to her should she refuse to do as was asked. Thereafter, the threats were then directed to you and, therefore, it is *you* that she seeks to protect, not herself."

A coldness wrapped around Matthew's heart, squeezing painfully. "Someone has threatened me?"

Lady Catherine nodded.

"And it is because she wishes to protect me that she does what is being asked of her which is, I presume, pushing back from the connection we shared? She is no longer able to be as closely acquainted as we once were?"

With a small shake of her head, Lady Catherine spread out her hands. "I think this is all that I can tell you, Lord Downfield. To say more would be unfair of me, for Lady Sarah trusts me as her friend and I fear that even this is betraying her trust. Though I speak so simply because I do not want her to lose whatever happiness she might have had with you."

Matthew offered her a small, wry smile. "Even though I have displeased you very often? You still think me worthy of being connected to Lady Sarah?"

It took a few moments for Lady Catherine to consider his question but, after a short while, she nodded. "Yes, I think that you are," she said, quietly. "You have changed, certainly, but you care for Sarah a great deal. I can see that in you and I know that you will come to value her all the more as the days go forward. That is why I must beg of you to do all you can to protect her, to break through this dark evil which has been forced upon her. I wish that I could say or do more but I do not think it would be right."

Matthew nodded. "I understand and I am grateful to you," he said, quietly. "I have told her that I consider this the fourth mystery, the final one which will bring an end to it all – and, as I hope, bring us back together again. I do not deserve it, I do not deserve *her*, Lord knows, but I will do all that I can to prove myself to her – no matter how long it takes."

At this, Lady Catherine smiled, though it still held a good deal of sadness within it. "Then I think you shall succeed, Lord Downfield, though it may take some time. Might I also suggest that you discover which of your acquaintances and friends have been speaking of Lady Sarah?"

Matthew frowned. "Speaking of her?"

Lady Catherine nodded. "Yes, of course. Someone will have said something to this person pushing threats upon Lady Sarah. Someone who knows a good deal about Lady Sarah, who might know more than society is permitted to know."

A white hot rage rushed through Matthew as his hands clenched into fists, understanding what she meant. "You mean to say that this person threatened to reveal that she was a bluestocking?"

Lady Catherine nodded, putting a hand to Lord Rutherford's arm for support. "You must ask yourself who of your acquaintances knows such a thing about her and why they would say something like that to others," she finished, glancing up at Lord Rutherford. "I know for certain it will not be Lord Rutherford."

"No, it will not be," Matthew grated, his chest tight with anger. "But I believe that I know who it is."

***

"Thank you for coming."

Lord Dover and Lord Stephenson glanced at each other as Matthew beckoned them in, choosing not to rise from his study desk. Instead, he sat behind it, aware that he was pushing a rather austere exterior but thinking that such a thing might be precisely what these two supposed friends of his needed to see, if he was to get the truth.

"It is somewhat strange to be summoned like this," Lord Dover said, casting another glance to Lord Stephenson, who nodded in evident agreement. "We are friends, are we not? Why did you send such a stern note, demanding that we come to speak with you at this time?"

Matthew, who had informed each of the gentlemen that the other would be present, offered them both a small shrug. "It is precisely because this matter is so severe," he stated, as calmly as he could. "It relates to my life and my current acquaintances… and, in that regard, to one particular lady." He lifted an eyebrow but both gentlemen simply looked back at him, blank expressions on each face. "It is about Lady Sarah."

At this, both Lord Dover and Lord Stephenson immediately dropped their gaze and, after a moment, Lord Stephenson passed one hand over his eyes.

"Something has happened," Matthew continued, when neither of his friends said a word. "Lady Sarah spoke to me at yesterday's ball and informed me that our acquaintance had to come to a most abrupt end. I was, of course, greatly upset at this for, even though I have not behaved as I ought to have done when it comes to the lady, I came to the realization of just how much of a fool I was being in treating her so poorly. I was thinking only of my reputation, of my standing in society rather than being connected to the lady that I have come to love." He spoke these last few words with as little emotion within them as he dared, only to find himself rather astonished to realize that yes, he *was* in love with Lady Sarah. It was more than just affection, more than just a small desire to draw closer to her. There was a depth to his feelings which he had never either experienced or identified before and that, Matthew recognized, was love.

"Love?" Lord Dover's lip curled. "Goodness, that is an odd idea. Why would you ever consider yourself in love? It cannot be wise to connect yourself to a young lady merely because of your feelings! There must be genuine consideration to her standing in society, to her –"

"You fear that because she is a bluestocking, I will, somehow, pass a shadow over my reputation."

Lord Dover nodded fervently. "Yes, and I know how much time you have put into protecting that, how much effort you have put into elevating yourself all the more. Society regards you as one of the greatest gentlemen in all of London, your reputation goes before you and then, to consider connecting yourself to Lady Sarah who, I am afraid, will soon be known as a bluestocking, seems quite foolish."

Matthew's jaw set tight though he did not allow his anger to show. It was anger mixed with shame, seeing that the words Lord Dover spoke were words that he himself understood. He recognized what it was that Lord Dover talked about, saw the importance of being seen by all of society in excellent standing, for it was what he himself had thought of for a very long time indeed.

But now, he turned his back on it entirely.

"I believe that it is *my* prerogative to deal with my reputation and my connections as I please, Lord Dover," he said, in a low tone, casting a look to Lord Stephenson who was still choosing not to look in Matthew's direction. "Both of you knew that Lady Sarah was something of a bluestocking. I believe I might even have told you – or one of you, at least – that there was concern in my heart as regarded her depth of learning and knowledge. That is to say that it came not from a concern about how much she knew and whether I would feel myself intimidated, but more from thoughts about the *ton* and how they might consider me. I can assure that I see that now as nothing but nonsense, a foolishness which I refuse to turn to. Alas, in that moment of understanding, I gained nothing more than confusion for Lady Sarah refused to return to my arm, stating that she must step back from me. And there must be a reason why."

Lord Stephenson's gaze darted to Matthew's for a moment. "Why do you think that either of us would know of it?"

"Because," Matthew said, slowly, choosing each word with great care. "Lady Catherine, Lady Sarah's closest friend, told me that the reason Lady Sarah can no longer tolerate my company is because she has been threatened, told that she must do this else suffer great consequences. Though, it seems, she has rejected that and said that she would not do as was asked, the reason she has now been coerced into doing so is simply because *I* have been threatened instead."

Lord Stephenson and Lord Dover blinked in confusion, then looked at each other. "I do not understand," Lord Dover said, slowly. "How can you be threatened?"

"It seems that this person has stated that, unless she does as has been demanded – that is, to stay away from me –

then my reputation will be ruined in some way. I cannot know what the specifics are of that, cannot tell whether this threat would truly be a great threat but, all the same, I find myself rather troubled. To hear that this has been placed upon Lady Sarah's shoulders is, I think, deeply concerning and it is for that purpose that I called you both here."

Both gentlemen looked at each other again. "Because you believe that one of us is responsible for this?"

Matthew nodded. "Yes," he said, simply.

"But how can that be?" Lord Stephenson asked, his expression dark with a sudden and obvious upset. "We are your friends, as you yourself have said, so why then would we do such a thing as that?"

"I do not mean that you have gone out deliberately and have spoken cruelly about either Lady Sarah or myself," Matthew explained, quickly, "but more to say that one of you is the cause of it all. One of you has spoken about Lady Sarah to someone else, one of you has spoken about her and her desire to learn, her desire to grow in knowledge. One of you has told another person that she is a bluestocking and that has now been used against her." He spread out his hands. "The only thing I desire to know now is which one of you did such a thing, not so that I can place the blame upon you but so that I can then discover who it was and why this person has gone on to determine that Lady Sarah must be set apart from me."

Lord Dover frowned only for his frown to pull into a scowl. Lord Stephenson, on the other hand, looked entirely blank, staring back at Matthew with rounded eyes, clearly a little confused over the matter.

Matthew knew at once who was responsible and, as such, turned his gaze back to Lord Dover, his eyebrows lifting in question.

Lord Dover rubbed one hand over his eyes and shook his head. "I did not mean... that is, I did not speak poorly of her deliberately. Do not think that I did. It was only because –"

"Who did you speak to about Lady Sarah?" Matthew interrupted sitting forward in his chair now, his hand thumping hard on the desk. "I do not need to know what was said nor how sorry you are for it all. The only thing I wish to know is *who* you spoke to."

With another heavy sigh, Lord Dover shook his head again, leaned his head back and looked straight at Matthew. "Lady Alice came to speak with me some evenings ago. She knew that you and I were well acquainted and, given that you were not showing her as much interest as she had hoped, she spoke with me about you."

A heavy weight pulled at Matthew's heart. "And so, you chose to speak about Lady Sarah? To the one person that you know would not think well of her?"

"I did not know that!" Lord Dover exclaimed, his eyes wide now. "I did not think for a moment that Lady Alice would do anything inconsiderate and indeed, I did not speak poorly about Lady Sarah, not in the way you might think. Instead, I simply shared that she was a young lady who was very well read, telling Lady Alice about the little mysteries that she has been playing out for you."

Scrubbing one hand over his face, Matthew let out a low groan. "And now Lady Alice has determined that, since I am not showing her the attentions she clearly requires, she is to force me into that situation regardless of my own thoughts and considerations. I am to do whatever *she* wants from me and she will go about it in any way she can."

"And what is worse," Lord Stephenson put in, sending Lord Dover a dark look, "it sounds as though she will threaten your standing also, if she does not get what she desires. It is almost as though if she cannot have you close to her, then she will not let anyone else have you either!"

"Precisely," Matthew growled, as Lord Dover hung his head, clearly ashamed of what he had done. "How could you do this, Lord Dover? I thought that you would know better than to speak ill in such a way!"

"I was a little in my cups," Lord Dover muttered, rubbing one hand over his eyes. "And I was also talking to the daughter of a Duke! I confess that I was a little overwhelmed. I wanted her to think well of me, I wanted her to think that I was a gentleman of note – much as you did – and in that regard, I spoke when I ought not to have done. It is perhaps too much to expect you to forgive me so quickly but I am truly sorry for what has been done."

Matthew scowled, finding his anger still present but, with it, an understanding of all that Lord Dover had done for he had been precisely the same for such a long time. "It will come, in time," he muttered, dismissively cutting through the air between them with one hand. "But for the moment, I must find a way to tell Lady Sarah all that I know, to tell her that all will be well... and to somehow prevent Lady Alice from speaking lies about either the lady or myself."

"Though does such a thing matter?"

Hearing the question in Lord Stephenson's voice, Matthew lifted his eyebrows in surprise. "I beg your pardon?"

"Why should such things matter? If you are determined that you will connect yourself to the lady, if you are quite certain that you will draw close to her regardless, then will it matter what Lady Alice says?"

Opening his mouth to speak, to state that yes, it certainly *did* matter, Matthew closed it again as he began to understand what it was that his friend meant. "I do not want her reputation or my own to be damaged unnecessarily," he said, slowly, "but nor do I want Lady Sarah to think that being a bluestocking is something that I wish to be hidden from them all. You are quite right, Lord Stephenson. Not a great deal should matter to me in that regard though I still want to make sure that I can do all that I can to protect her."

His friend smiled at him, though Lord Dover was still looking away, a dark expression on his face. "Then I am certain you shall succeed! If it is of any use to you, I shall do whatever I can to support you in this. It is clear that you have a happiness in reach."

"I would be glad of it."

Lord Dover glanced at him. "If there is a way that I can make amends, then you know that I would be willing to do so."

"I do," Matthew said, seeing the upset on his friend's face and allowing it to steal some of his anger away. "I have some thinking to do but, when the time comes, I will need you both to be as delighted about my engagement as you can – and to throw aside any rumours or whispers about Lady Sarah being a bluestocking."

Lord Dover and Lord Stephenson's eyes both widened at exactly the same time. For a few minutes, nothing was said until, with a clearing of his throat, Lord Stephenson spoke quietly.

"Engagement? You want to marry her?"

"Yes," Matthew said firmly, with a determination which filled him with excitement rather than fear or dread. "I am certain that I want to do so. To have her by my side, to have her as my bride so that we are never separated again... I can think of nothing better."

Epilogue

"Why will you not step out into society?"

Sarah looked away as her mother marched into the drawing room, her arms akimbo.

"Why will you not?" Lady Harcastle demanded, though Sarah kept her gaze pulled away from her mother. "I hear that you have told the maid you will not be attending the ball this evening and that is the third one you have missed in the last few days!"

Hearing the silence waiting for her answer, Sarah lifted her shoulders and let them fall. "I do not feel particularly eager to step out into society."

Lady Harcastle let out an exclamation. "That is your only reason?"

"It is."

She shook her head. "Then it is nothing serious, is it?"

Sarah looked to her mother, her melancholy like a deep and constant pain which she could not escape from. "I – I cannot say much more than that, Mama."

Lady Harcastle's eyes sharpened. "You sit here and sulk and will not tell me why it is that you are so troubled?"

"I am not sulking, Mama," Sarah answered, her voice a little broken as emotions sought to capture her again. "I can assure you, I am quite well. I simply am rather tired from the weeks of interactions with others and would prefer a day or two simply to rest." She tried to smile but her mouth would not do as she asked it, instead sitting in a flat line which tried its hardest to pull downwards, given the sorrow within her heart.

"My dear." Lady Harcastle came to sit beside Sarah, her hand reaching to take Sarah's in her own. "You are troubled by something – or by someone – but you will not tell me what it is! I know that there has been some upset between us given your love of reading and what your father and I have forbidden, but I do hope that you have not held any such thing against us."

"Of course I have not," Sarah answered, recalling how she had been doing her best to not only free herself from her parents' demands but had been bold enough to step into a bookshop on more than one occasion. That last thought, however, swept her back into the memory of being in Lord Downfield's arms and with that came a surge of pain. It was so sharp, Sarah caught her breath and looked away, hating that tears came into her eyes as she fought hard to hide them from her mother.

"Why will you not tell me, then?" Lady Harcastle asked, her own voice a little tremulous. "I feel as though there is a great chasm between us and I cannot breach it!"

Sarah closed her eyes and, much to her relief, tears did not drip down her cheeks. "Please, Mama, believe me when I say there is nothing that I need to speak with you about, nothing that I need to share." She offered her mother a small smile, opening her eyes though her vision was a little blurred around the edges. "I shall return to society and all will be well. I simply need a day or two to rest." She smiled all the brighter though the pain in her heart was so great, it was almost impossible to do so for long. She dared not speak about Lord Downfield, knowing that there would follow nothing but questions and whispers of hope – neither of which Sarah could offer her mother. She could not give her answers, could not even hope that things might improve between Lord Downfield and herself for she had made a decision, had stepped back from him and now Lady Alice would be given everything she wanted.

"Please, Sarah, if there is –"

The door to the drawing room flew open and Sarah caught her breath, her eyes flaring wide as Lord Downfield, the very gentleman she had been thinking of, walked into the room, his eyes blazing with a light which Sarah had never seen in his expression before.

"Lady Harcastle, Lady Sarah, forgive the interruption but I could not stop myself and wait for the footman to bring you news of my arrival and hope of calling upon you," he said, his voice echoing around the room. His eyes sought hers, a softness surrounding them which spoke tenderness to Sarah's heart. "Sarah, there is much I must say to you."

"Whatever is the matter?"

Sarah got to her feet – as did her mother – as Lord Harcastle came into the room.

"I heard a loud noise and thought there was something untoward going on, only to see now that it is only that you have a gentleman caller, Sarah." Lord Harcastle harrumphed and then came a little further into the room. "Lord Downfield, is it not?"

"Yes, it is." Lord Downfield inclined his head. "I am glad you have arrived, Lord Harcastle, for there is something I wish to say in your hearing, and in the hearing of your wife." He took in a deep breath and butterflies erupted in Sarah's stomach, seeing how he nodded to himself as though he were determined now to say whatever was in his mind. She had no thought, not even the smallest imagining of what it might be and yet her whole body was filled with both excitement and worry.

"Then what it is?" Lady Harcastle asked, exchanging a glance with Sarah. "Is it about my daughter?"

"It is." Lord Downfield smiled at Sarah, spreading out his hands. "I know that you are a bluestocking, Lady Sarah. I know that, Lord Harcastle, and I think it the most wonderful thing."

Sarah's eyes burned with tears as she clasped her hands tight together in front of her, sinking back down onto the couch behind her.

"I understand that you have been afraid that there may be those within the *ton* who would think poorly of your daughter but I can assure you that I do not. I think that her learning, her love of reading and her delight in furthering her knowledge is a trait which I find utterly wonderful. Indeed, I think it so remarkable, I should like to hear more of what she has learned. I would like to know what books she is reading at present, I would like to get into discussion about all such things as that. In short, Lord and Lady Harcastle, I would like to court your daughter with the expectation that engagement shall soon follow."

It was as though the entire world froze in time for just a few moments. Sarah did not even take a breath, staring at Lord Downfield as he spoke with astonishment rattling through her. How could he ask her parents such a thing? How could he speak to *her* of such a desire when she had forced herself back from him? Clearly, he did not understand what it was that troubled her so, did not fully recognize all that would follow if he dared do such a thing and yet, in that, Sarah's heart softened as Lord Downfield smiled at her.

"Well... this is most unexpected." Lord Harcastle ran one hand over his chin, then shrugged. "I did not think – that is to say, I did not expect – that any gentleman would ever think well of such a thing. I have told Sarah repeatedly that she is not to speak of her learning, she is not to tell anyone of the books she so adores and she is certainly not to be seen in a bookshop and yet, somehow, you have discovered it?"

"I have," Lord Downfield stated, unequivocally. "I

believe that, as our connection has grown, Lady Sarah has wanted to be quite clear as to who she is so that *I* can understand her a little more. I have been appreciative of that also, for it would not have been good for me to seek to court a young lady who I did not really know. All that I must ask now, Lord Harcastle, is whether or not I might be able to get your permission to court Lady Sarah, knowing what it is that I seek from such a connection?"

Sarah's heart began to beat furiously, protest on her lips. It was not that she did not want to accept such an offer, was not that she did not desire to be close with him but feared that, should she do such a thing, the consequences which would follow would be dreadful indeed.

"It would have to be with my daughter's agreement, of course," Lord Harcastle said, looking to Sarah for the first time. "But I have no concern in that regard and do, of course, grant you my permission."

"Wonderful." Lord Downfield was grinning, a light shining in his eyes but Sarah could feel nothing but fear curling in her stomach. It was as though happiness and delight was trying to break through but it could not, such was her concern.

"Please, Lord Downfield, I – "

"Might I be permitted to spend a few minutes alone with Lady Sarah? It would only be for a few moments, of course and the door would be left wide open," Lord Downfield smiled at Sarah and then looked to Lord Harcastle. "I can promise you that I will be entirely proper. I only wish to convey to Lady Sarah the depth of my feelings."

Lord Harcastle's eyebrows lifted again but, after a moment, he nodded. With a look to Lady Harcastle, both he and his wife stepped out of the room, leaving Sarah and Lord Downfield alone.

Silence reigned for a moment.

"Sarah," Lord Downfield breathed, coming closer to her though Sarah could not bring herself even to rise, her heart clamoring within her. "I cannot spend the rest of my life without you, forced away from you by the simple demands of a lady of quality."

She blinked in astonishment. "You know who it is who has made such demands?"

"Your fourth mystery, whether you meant it to be or not." He tilted his head. "Lady Alice has demanded this of you? She wants me to consider *her* rather than you, does she not?"

With a lump in her throat, Sarah nodded, tears beginning to burn in her eyes.

"And she threatened you?"

"She told me I had to step back from you, else she would tell everyone that I was a bluestocking, would make certain that society looked down upon me."

Lord Downfield reached out and took her hand, before coming to sit beside her, looking deeply into her eyes. "And then, instead, she threatened me?"

With a tight chest, Sarah nodded. "It seems as though she is determined enough that, should she not be given what she wants, she will then go ahead and injure you also. It is as though society must look down upon you so that she will, in some dark way, feel triumphant."

His hand squeezed hers. "And so, because you were so determined to protect me, you said that you would do such a thing? Even though you did not want to?"

"Even though I did not want to. It caused me immense pain to do as was demanded, I can assure you," Sarah managed to choke out, her tears now falling to her cheeks. "My dear Downfield, to hear you say such things to my parents caused me both great joy and great fear! What will become of you should you do this?"

Lord Downfield shrugged his shoulders. "I care not."

"But... " She gazed back at him, trying to understand. "But you have always cared about reputation. I have seen it since the moment we first met, since we began our acquaintance. You have pulled away from it, yes, but – "

"And now I pull away from it entirely," he interrupted, speaking so gently that Sarah's heart squeezed with a surge of love for the gentleman before her. "You are worth more than a thousand members of the *ton,* all giving me their opinions. I have realised once and for all how foolish I was to ever turn away from you, to look instead to the views of society and to seek out *their* consideration rather than yours."

Sarah swallowed hard, her breathing growing quicker as she looked back into his eyes, seeing that he meant every word.

"I have treated you abysmally," he finished, shaking his head and looking away, regret written into every part of his expression. "When I kissed you in the bookshop, I should have told you of my feelings then and there, I should have begged for you to consider me, to consider what might be a happy and contented future between us. Instead, I retreated, I hid and I found myself utterly lost in my own confusion. How grateful I am for Lord Rutherford for pulling me from it! He showed me what I already knew, what I had held deep within my heart... and that is, that I have fallen in love with you and that, Sarah, *that* is all that matters."

Sarah closed her eyes and smiled, though tears began to rain down on her cheeks. Lord Downfield made a noise of concern in his throat but Sarah opened her eyes, reached out her hands and cupped his face, feeling a gentle roughness at her fingertips. "It tore me apart to break apart from you," she whispered, hoarsely. "I love you in return. I did not want to be separated from you but I was too afraid, afraid of all that could be brought against you if I did not do what she said."

"And I was afraid that I would lose you," he said, fervently. "Can you truly be willing enough to give me your heart, when I have let you down so many times?"

She nodded, laughing softly as his eyes flared in obvious relief and joy. "My dear Downfield, I have seen you change, I have seen how altered you have become. Not only that, you have proven yourself to me by stepping into this room and declaring to my parents that you know not only that I am a bluestocking but that you are thrilled by that! To know that you support my endeavors, that you will not insist on pushing that away from me has made my heart so glad."

"I love you for who you are," he promised, softly. "So, when it comes to this, will you court me, Sarah?" He paused, then tilted his head just a little. "More than that, I think. Will you marry me?"

Sarah's heart burst with happiness. "I cannot refuse you, Downfield."

His eyes lit up. "Then you will?"

"I will."

He leaned closer to her then, his lips finding hers and, in that sweet and gentle kiss, Sarah felt all of the pain within her healing, the wounds from Lady Alice no longer troubling her. She knew for certain that, no matter what Lady Alice threatened, there would be nothing now to prevent their happiness. She sighed happily as the kiss came to an end, her forehead resting against his for just a moment.

"I think I have solved all of your mysteries now, have I not?"

She laughed then, her hands going to the back of his

neck, her fingers brushing through his hair. "I believe that you have. There can be nothing between us now."

"Indeed," he grinned, pulling back just a little so he could look into her eyes. "I think that we need not concern ourselves one iota over what Lady Alice might say. We shall announce our engagement and, if she chooses to do as she has threatened, then I believe that the *ton* will not believe her words. But even if they do, that will not be a consideration on my mind. All I will be thinking of will be our marriage, our future happiness and our life together."

Sarah smiled gently, tears of joy in her eyes as her heart finally settled, wrapped now in the love offered from Lord Downfield. "As shall I," she said, as he began to lean towards her again. "I love you, Downfield."

His lips brushed hers. "Just as I love you."

THE END

Printed in Great Britain
by Amazon